UMEED INDIA
with
VIRENDER SEHWAG

EPIC Television Channel is the flagship factual entertainment offering from IN10 Media—a network with diverse interests in the media and entertainment sector. It is an India-centric, content-driven destination that has redefined the genre by being the only native Hindi-language infotainment channel. With a reputation for excellence in showcasing premium factual content that celebrates, explores, discovers and inspires India through untold stories, facts and possibilities, over the years, EPIC Television Channel has been bestowed with several accolades, including the prestigious PromaxBDA Award across various categories, the Indian Television Academy Award for the show *Stories by Rabindranath Tagore* and the Asian Rainbow Television Award for the show *Umeed India*.

UMEED INDIA
with
VIRENDER SEHWAG

GUTS, GLORY...AND GOLD!

RUPA

Published by
Rupa Publications India Pvt. Ltd 2019
7/16, Ansari Road, Daryaganj
New Delhi 110002

Sales centres:
Allahabad Bengaluru Chennai
Hyderabad Jaipur Kathmandu
Kolkata Mumbai

ISBN: 978-93-5333-618-9

First impression 2019

10 9 8 7 6 5 4 3 2 1

Transcription and translation by Malobika Chatterjee

CONTENTS

1

AVTAR SINGH

An Olympic medal is like a new life. It is like you are given a new identity. If you win an Olympic medal, it is as though your parents will also achieve renown, and so will your country.

People must be wondering what I am doing dressed up as a judo player surrounded by all these players. What Delhi is to politics, Eden Gardens is to cricket, what Mumbai is to Bollywood, Gurdaspur is to judo. The city is known as the judo capital of India; a bunch of talented players have emerged from here. One such player, who is our hope in the next Olympics, is Avtar Singh.

And we have come here especially to meet this talent.

Virender Sehwag: What meaning does judo hold for you, Avtar Singh ji?

Avtar Singh: It is a part of my life and my life depends on judo.

V.S.: What if judo is removed from your life?

A.S.: Then it becomes zero, doesn't it? There is nothing for me then.

V.S.: How and when did you start learning judo?

A.S.: As a kid I was very naughty, in fact, you can say I was almost a bully. At home, I would fight and squabble a lot; I was a stubborn child and the entire day was spent in throwing tantrums for one thing or the other. Kids my age were scared of me, so one day, my father had an idea. He told me that instead of wasting my energy on trivial matters I should concentrate on some sport, and that is how judo was introduced into my life (smiling). Initially, for a couple of months, it was fine and I was excited as kids usually are with a new sport. But then I lost interest and left judo. Only after leaving judo did I realize how much I missed it. Then I decided to continue with judo. When I resumed the sport it felt so good. I went on to play state, nationals and then seniors. Someone then told me that India has no medal in judo in the Olympics. I then decided to make that my target—to get an Olympic medal.

V.S.: Do you know that I have enrolled my children for judo and karate so that it benefits them while playing cricket? This is because in judo your whole body is used, and each and every body muscle is utilized. It strengthens your muscles; and also by using different techniques, you develop a certain kind of mindset. Okay, tell me now, did you actually think of quitting judo in 2008?

A.S.: This was in 2008–09 and I was in Class XI, still in school.

The club where I used to train had no coach, and then one day, while I was at my game and actually winning it, I was forced to lose. I was a child then and it broke me completely. I went home disheartened and told my father, I am quitting the game. The situation of being asked to lose was killing me from inside and I was sure I would not be able to take it anymore. I still remember the conversation with my father that day and he told me to not lose heart so easily. He told me to stay firm and that this was the beginning of the game of my life. He told me this was the time to show everyone who had criticized me or not taken me seriously; this was the time to show who I really was. I went on to participate in the Commonwealth Games and won a gold medal. Things changed for me that day onwards.

V.S.: I had heard about politics in sports. And when I talk to these athletes and they tell me about all the problems they had to go through, I feel very bad. If the athletes have to deal with such issues and the good players are thus demotivated, then our expectations from them are wrong.

Moving on to my next question, when you were a child, did you lend a helping hand to your parents?

A.S.: Yes I did, but my mind was only on sports (smiling). I would feel like going and playing some sport all the time instead of helping them! I would feel like having some fun with friends too; even now I feel like that sometimes.

V.S.: So what were the household chores in which you helped your parents?

A.S.: Like doing some work in the fields—cutting up the grass, helping with threshing the wheat, etc.—things that one does while leading a village life. Nowadays, sometimes I miss all that; sometimes my heart longs for those kind of activities.

V.S.: What kind of a student were you?

A.S.: I was quite all right till Classes V and VI (shy and smiling).

V.S.: But there was no exam system then (smirking).

A.S.: No sir, exams used to take place.

V.S.: For Classes V and VI?

A.S.: Yes sir, exams were there.

V.S.: What is your educational qualification? Did you complete your graduation?

A.S.: Yes, I have completed my graduation.

V.S.: Then you felt that you must get a job...and you...?

A.S.: Yes. After Class XII itself, I joined the Punjab Police as a constable. I thought I should have some financial stability.

V.S.: After that you participated in the Olympics and won a lot of accolades, attributing to your wonderful performance, and your parents also came into the limelight. What were your feelings when you brought so much honour to your parents?

A.S.: It is the best feeling that any child can have. Because of me, my parents were honoured and they got to see the world. Before this my parents had not stepped out of Amritsar; they had not even been to Delhi. And here they were, with me on an international flight. The way my parents felt when they were with me on this flight was matchless...it was priceless, and this in itself was an achievement for me.

V.S.: And so, with your increased recognition and fame, are you getting many marriage proposals (smiling)?

A.S.: Yes, even yesterday there was one (smiling shyly).

V.S.: So, did she pass or fail?

A.S.: So far, all have failed. Actually I am only thinking about the Olympics right now; I am only concentrating on my game. The aim is to get that medal. Marriage is bound to happen sometime. But let me achieve something first. Marriage can wait.

V.S.: Did you play any other sport besides judo in your childhood?

A.S.: Yes, I used to play kancha (marbles).

V.S.: How good a player were you?

A.S.: Oh! I was quite good (laughing).

V.S.: Talking about marbles, you have also reminded me of my childhood. I also used to play with marbles a lot and was quite good at it, though I used to get a lot of scolding from my parents for wasting my time on marbles (smiling).

A.S.: Sir, even I was scolded a lot. In fact, I was scolded for playing cricket and wasting my time (laughing).

V.S.: Oh! So you were scolded for playing cricket! I think it is now time to meet your parents (smiling).

I have now come to meet Avtar's parents who are sitting

on a charpoy under a tree. There is a vast expanse of fields in the background. Avtar's father is dressed simply in a shirt and a pair of trousers and his mother in salwar kameez and dupatta. I will ask both of them about Avtar as a child.

Tell me about your son Avtar. How was he as a kid? Was he naughty, mischievous?

Mrs Singh: He was a happy child. He was never angry about anything. He was naughty but a happy-go-lucky kind of person. I can say that he never took anything to heart, and in some sense, he was not serious about life.

V.S.: I want to ask both of you—you have seen Avtar as a school-going kid as well as an international player. Do you see any change in him as a person? Is he any different from what he was earlier and what he is now?

Mr Singh: (laughing) I don't think so.

Mrs Singh: At home, he is just like any other kid. He will roam around the house, making noise and commotion. You know how kids behave in their homes. But I tell him (smiling), 'Avtar, please don't make so much noise. Soon you will leave the house for your sports tour and then the house will be empty and I will miss your voice.'

V.S.: (laughing) Okay. I have heard that you broke into your savings when Avtar Singh went to the Turkish Grand for the first time. Is it true?

Mr Singh: Yes...yes...

V.S.: ...all the money that you had, whatever you had earned and saved? Please tell me more about that.

Mr Singh: Whatever I had saved, I spent on Avtar Singh. I never looked back or thought twice—whether it would be worth it or not. I even took help from my friends to ensure that Avtar doesn't face any problems.

V.S.: But, were you never afraid thinking 'what if he does not succeed' after investing everything?

Mr Singh: See, he is our child and everything is for him. After all, he is doing something in life, or is at least trying to. As parents, we should help him. He is not gambling, right (smiling)? It is very good to see that he is working very hard. I still remember the phone call he made from Delhi. 'Papa, I have qualified,' he said, and these were golden words to my ears. I still remember that moment and I was very happy. It is actually impossible to express what I felt then.

V.S. How fortunate is the father who is known by the achievements of his son.

Mr Singh: Very true! He is a very talented son. He has participated in the Olympics, has gone to the highest level of the game. I had never thought that he would go to Rio, but see, he went. We had never dreamt of going to Rio, but see, our son took both of us to a foreign country. We are very fortunate to have him as our son.

V.S.: I am sure the children in your village must be greatly influenced by Avtar Singh. I am sure they aspire to be like him one day. They all want to be Avtar Singh, isn't it?

Mr Singh: All the kids in the district know that Avtar Singh went to Rio. They have this feeling that they can also do it and be famous. He is an inspiration for them.

Mrs Singh: That is why all the children want to learn judo so that they can be like Avtar.

V.S.: That is what I want to ask—do children here say that they also want to be Avtar Singh?

Mrs Singh: Yes. They come to me and ask me, can I play judo? Can I be like Avtar? And I tell them, why not, go ahead (smiling).

V.S.: This is what a champion can do. Inspire so many youngsters to follow him. Every kid in Gurdaspur wants to follow Avtar Singh's footsteps and be like him.

But Avtar Singh has not forgotten the man because of whom he has achieved what he has—his coach.

A.S.: For me, my coach is everything, because ever since I met him, he not only taught me but also ingrained in me everything that I did not know—like how to live in a foreign country, how to cope with different climates, how to come back from a losing game, how to rise to the occasion while participating in a big tournament. I share a special relationship with my coach. When we are on the mat he is like a teacher, and when I am not training he is like a friend. I can share everything with my coach.

V.S.: A coach is everything to a student. He is as affectionate and loving as a mother or a father; stands by one's side like a friend; gives good advice like a brother and secures one's future like a mentor. That is the kind of relationship Avtar Singh has with his coach, Yashpal Singh Solanki, recipient of the Arjun Award. It is now time to meet the man himself.

V.S.: How important is the role of a coach who guides one along the right path and changes the life of his protégé?

Yashpal Singh: Sir, in my opinion, a coach should be everything. Not only on the mat, but also in the life of a player. He should be like a parent, a senior and an elder brother. He inculcates values in his protégé. A good bonding between a mentor and the mentee surpasses even a blood relation—like I spend more time with my students than with my own children! These kids are my extended family.

V.S.: How and where did you meet Avtar Singh and what did you see in him that made you decide to take him on as a student?

Y.S.: It was in 2011 that I met Avtar for the first time. At that time, I was actively playing and was participating in the Commonwealth Games. I was in the senior team and he was in the junior. During the last few years, when I was retiring, he was my opponent. Since he was my opponent, I knew what his strength was. I was very skilled, and it was practically impossible for anyone to score points off me. When I played against him it seemed to me that this boy was not afraid at all! So I took him into the team and ever since then—from December 2012 to this moment—we have been together.

V.S.: How different is Avtar Singh from other players?

Y.S.: Physically, he is the tallest in his category and his fitness level is among the best in the world. In fact, it is at par with the international players. He is a very good soul. The most striking factor about him is that he is very daring. He is so daring that even when he is going to fight against a world champion, there is no sense of panic in him. Yes, he is also very emotional, and that can be counted as his strength. However, sometimes, because of this emotional nature, he breaks down completely. During such distressing times, he needs a brother or a senior to be with him and I am right there beside him. Otherwise, there is never any sense of fright or the desire to retreat in him. This is a unique characteristic in him.

V.S.: Do you remember any particular incident about Avtar Singh?

Y.S.: Yes. There are some people who work against Avtar Singh. They plot to defeat him and try and disturb his mind. During these times, I wonder whether these people are on India's side or not.

V.S.: And this has happened once?

Y.S.: Not once, innumerable times. At such times, I wonder how to support Avtar; I become so demotivated myself. This has happened a great number of times (tries to hide his tears).

V.S.: I hope that in future this doesn't happen and Avtar gets support from each and every quarter. But you also know there is a saying in our country that people down below tend to try and pull down those rising to great heights—it happens in cricket and in other sports as well.

Okay, tell me now about your game plan for the coming Olympics.

Y.S.: We have categorized our training into two divisions. For the first two years i.e. 2017 and 2018—we tried for maximum training exposure so that our base would become strong. For these two years, there was more of training and less participation in competitions. We were getting the techniques right without caring about our ranking because, honestly speaking, rankings in 2020 will depend upon the events we participate in 2018 and 2019. So, for the next two years, there is maximum competition. This ensures exposure at two levels—training and competition; the more we participate in events close to the Olympics, the less will be the anxiety. Performing well in the Olympics will seem easy.

V.S.: Thank you very much for sharing your experiences. All our good wishes that you will proceed in the right direction, and we wish that in the 2020 Olympics, you will definitely bring home a medal.

Y.S.: Thank you very much, sir. We hope that whatever we have undertaken is fulfilled and we see our *tiranga* rising and flying high at the Olympics. Nothing else matters.

V.S.: More than a game of strength, judo is a battle of technique and energy. On the judo mat, there is a constant test of physical and mental strength. And preparations for such a test is no mean task. This is why Avtar Singh is going through tough training each day. Today, let us also become a part of this training.

Y.S.: The first session begins at 6 in the morning. 8 a.m. is the time for our general conditioning, speed and endurance. This training is separate from the training on mats.

A.S.: First, we begin with warm up, stretching etc. Two or three rounds of 400 m; then short sprints and jumps, as many times as possible.

Y.S.: You see, the main idea behind any training is to develop speed with explosive power. At 10.30 a.m., we come to the mat and there the focus is on techniques. Avtar attacks well and is generally aggressive, but his finishing is not too good. That is his weak point and we are working towards it. Then, in the evening session, the techniques learnt in the morning session are applied. This part of the training is called the Randori session. In other words, they are free sessions and we try to fight. The plus and minus points are both observed, so that the mistakes that have been noted are corrected the very next day.

A.S.: It is my height that gives me an advantage; because in India, in fact, in the world, I am the tallest in the heavyweight category. The reach that it gives me is a very big advantage.

Y.S.: His leg strength and speed is very good; he uses it very smartly, to his advantage. However, we are trying to improve it so much so that we do not allow our opponents even to stand.

V.S.: Tell me, Avtar Singh—did you ever think that you would qualify for the Rio Olympics?

A.S.: Well, sir, in 2011, I had started participating in the singles. And from there this feeling entered my mind that there are a lot of players who have played international matches, and so my target was to achieve something more and do better than them. Then I met coach sir and my thinking at that time aligned with his method of training, his discipline and temperament. So it is my good fortune that I met him and in return what he has got is a good student (laughs). We both complement each other.

V.S.: So, it's like a Sachin-Sehwag pair in cricket (big smile). If they do well, India has a chance (smiles again).

A.S.: Sir is a very positive person. There are times when I get demotivated or maybe become a bit complacent or satisfied with my performance. There are times when I say, chalo, let's leave it this time and we can try next time. But sir will always say, 'No. Why not this time?' He keeps pushing the limits, and that is what keeps me going and aspiring to achieve something big. He always says everything is going to be just fine. In his dictionary there is nothing negative. It is this trait of his that has brought me so far.

V.S.: You are so right, Avtar. I always say that this is the characteristic of a good player—a player who moves ahead in life from being good to great. Such a player has a very positive mindset. It is always a 'yes' from the word go and that is why such players excel.

V.S.: So, my last question to you is—what meaning does an Olympic medal have for you?

A.S.: An Olympic medal is like a new life. It is as if you are given a new identity. My parents will achieve renown and so will my country. That is a major factor. The peace and calm, which that medal will bring, cannot be derived from anything else.

V.S.: This is something great that Avtar Singh has said—the thrill of achievement and peace that this medal will bring cannot be achieved from anything else. Even getting all the wealth in this world will not bring this. Not just Avtar Singh, every athlete who participates in the Olympics has this feeling. I am not that fortunate because the sport that I play is not included in the Olympics. But Avtar Singh, you are lucky and have an opportunity to bring home a gold, silver or bronze medal for India.

Friends, I have great hopes from Avtar Singh. That is why I believe that in the upcoming Olympics India will get a medal in judo. I also wish that sports should be made part of the school curriculum, and especially judo, because the foundations of this sport is based on respect. It is a game that should be inculcated in our belief system.

Avtar Singh, all the best from all of us. Jai Hind!

2

OM PRAKASH SINGH KARHANA

When a player bows down on the podium to accept a medal, all Indians look up with a great deal of pride. When the action over the course of a match heightens dramatically, Indians cheering for their player and team skip a heartbeat. When any sportsperson is on the verge of victory, the entire country prays for them. A single player unites the whole of India. An opportunity to know such players in whom are vested the hopes and aspirations of our country is brought to you by Umeed India.

It is easy to spot Om Prakash Karhana or O.P.K. in a crowd...standing at 6 feet 7 inches and weighing 135 kg, with a boyish disposition and an infectious energy. But what makes this titan from Gurgaon stand out is his potential for the unexplored sport, shot-put, which earned him a bronze medal in the 20th Asian Athletics Championships (2013) and a gold medal at the 6th Asian Indoor Athletics Championships (2014) among other accolades to his credit. In this interview, I explore the life experiences, dedication and daily routine of this uber-talented shot-putter, O.P.K. Know how O.P.K.'s highly supportive family and his coach Bhupinder Singh helped him create the national record of distance 20.69 m in shot-put.

But before that, let me try a hand at this iron ball.

(Virender Sehwag is seen on a playground with a shot-put. He tries to throw the iron ball and it goes up to a metre and a half.)

Virender Sehwag: It seems to be impossible for me to throw this very far. What amazes me is how far our star athlete Om Prakash Karhana manages to throw it—up to 20 m!

Om Prakash Karhana: This is how we teach, sir! However, your attempt was very good. It was a good effort. The strength, speed and whatever else is needed for this—you gave it a good shot.

This is the putting style, placing it on our shoulder near the neck, and then throwing it.

V.S.: There is a saying, *jiska kaam usi ko saajhe,* meaning the person should only do the work that suits him, else they will make a fool out of themselves. I should not even have tried to pick it up or throw it—that is his task and I should have left it to him. Thank you very much, Om Prakash ji, for giving us your time and talking to us. Now tell me something—at home, my kids play Candy Crush. They have the impression that Candy Crush is especially exported for them; and I play cricket. What is this game of shot-put?

O.P.K.: This is a game for men (bursts out laughing).

V.S.: Accepted that it is a game for men. Out here people are mainly obsessed with cricket, or they remain engrossed in football and tennis. But what happens in a game of shot-put? How is it played and how much hard work is needed?

O.P.K.: Shot-put is basically an iron ball. It is 7 kg and 226 gm. It is a shot-put—which means you have to position it and then throw. Further, it is thrown from within a 2-m circle. You have to throw it only from within the circle, and if you step outside that, it is taken to be a foul. There are basically two techniques—one is the rotational technique and the other is the Parry O'Brien technique. Normally, people use the rotational technique.

V.S.: So, to pick up this 16-pound iron ball is no mean task. Is it similar to that famous Sunny Deol dialogue (laughs)! So, how much would your hand be?

O.P.K.: Sir, at the moment I do bench presses with at least 250 kg.

V.S.: I have also heard that your father got you out of a Hindi-medium school and put you into an English-medium school. Were you happy with that?

O.P.K.: Actually, my mother had forced my father, saying, 'He is good at studies, but he doesn't focus,' because the atmosphere is not suitable. The village ambience is for playing. That is why she forced me to go to the school for the children of defence personnel, saying to my father, 'Take him there.' So when he took me there, to the Army Public School in Simla, it was English-medium. There

I was in the limelight because I was always a good student. I was always among the first three in class. Then it occurred to me that my desire for scoring high marks was taking a back seat. So, during that period, the basketball team in my school was good, and I started playing basketball. So, what would happen when a basketball match would be played in school—was that we would be leading by three quarters, and children and girls would also be watching. My team, among all those who remained, their focus would change. In the last quarter, we lost 2 matches. Due to lack of focus and for a little show-off, our team started attempting 3-pointers from outside the range. We lost the last quarter by 10–12 points.

Right from the start I was very impatient, and I decided that it was impossible for me to play a team sport, and intended to take up an individual sport.

At the time I was beginning to develop some slight knowledge about shot-put and started doing what was required.

V.S.: At what crossroads in your life did you decide that you would make shot-put the main focus in your life?

O.P.K.: What happened was that when, in the course of playing in school, I brought home the national medal, Lalit Bhanot ji saw me and talked to me. He felt that I was a genuine talent. He began asking, 'How far do you throw?' Actually, then even I did not know how far I was throwing! So I answered, 'I throw for quite a distance.'

'Very far? Can you throw 20 m?'

I replied, 'Yes, I throw 20 m.'

V.S.: At that time he insisted you should throw up to 20 m. What then?

O.P.K.: Yes, in competitions—the next day there was a competition and I made it to about 17 m or something. It was close.

V.S.: O.P. had said 20 m in jest, but the record that was there, the national record, was 20.42. It was he who broke the record; and in my mind it was not once but two or three times, and his record was 20.69.

There are ups and downs in life. Unfortunately, when there is an injury, it means another set of problems. It also takes a lot of time to recover. You surely have gone through this also?

O.P.K.: You are also a sportsperson, and these things happen, and there are ups and downs in sports. In 2014, when I was going for the Asian Games, my standard throw was about 19 m, which is eligible for a medal. When I was about to throw above 19 m, my ankle twisted on both sides. It was just 8 or 10 days before the Games. Then I felt that everything was over. From there, my coach—Bhupinder Singh ji—his role became very important. It was just like a mother loving and nurturing her small child. He handled me with a lot of love. When I was angry and hurt, he patted me and said, 'Child, don't worry, your time will come.' Proceeding in this manner, now, after almost 2½ years, I am beginning to feel that fire in me again.

V.S.: It's like a child learning to walk again.

O.P.K.: Yes, absolutely!

V.S.: This kind of thing also happened to me once when I decided to retire in 2007. Then I talked to Sachin Tendulkar and told him that I was going to announce my retirement the next day. He stopped me and said that it was just a bad phase. Just like your coach, he made me sit down and had me eat something, talked to me and assured me that my bad form was just a bad patch and things would be fine again. Likewise, I hope your bad times are over and you will once again shine, and this time you will again bring an Olympics medal.

O.P.K.: Yes sir, gold, with world record...

V.S.: (intervenes) Gold with world record!

O.P.K.: Gold with world record—that is my target and only then will I be truly satisfied.

V.S.: Absolutely!

A guru or a mentor/coach is not compared to God for nothing. So, come, let us meet this God who helped put Omprakash on the world map—his guru, coach and inspiration, Sri Bhupinder Singh ji.

V.S.: How is O.P. as a student?

Bhupinder Singh: He is a very good student and extremely dedicated, committed and intelligent as well. There is a great deal of interest in training as much as possible and sometimes he has to be stopped from overdoing it. When he is stopped, he turns around and says, 'What is this? How can one become a world champion in this manner? How will I break records?'

V.S.: And you have to control him?

B.S.: Of course; it becomes too much. O.P.'s strongest point is continuous training. His biggest weakness is that he wants to do everything now. He has very little patience.

V.S.: Olympics is a very big event for everybody. So, how much pressure is there on you and O.P.? I mean, as the Olympics draws nearer, the pressure increases. Let me rephrase it, not exactly pressure, but expectations.

B.S.: Expectations should be there. If that is not there, there is nothing.

V.S.: If 125 crore people keep building up their expectations, pressure is bound to build up. What kind of training do you follow with O.P.?

B.S.: Training is a continuous process where you continue to try and do your best. The schedule is divided into cycles; cycles are then divided into years and years are taken into a 4–year schedule. For 6–7 years you have to remain fit. Suppose you are injured today, then you are just out.

V.S.: So we hope that O.P. remains fit and healthy till the Olympics and definitely brings home a medal.

B.S.: If you are looking at the Olympics as your target, then there appears to be no other contenders.

V.S.: There is only one person—O.P.!

We have heard about O.P.'s training programme from Bhupinder ji. Now, let us take a look at what a typical day in the life of O.P. is like.

O.P.K.: My day begins roughly around 5.30 a.m. Before leaving for training I have dry fruits, etc. Then I leave for training and after I reach there, the training starts at around

7.00 a.m. There are three types of training—first is general fitness, next is strength and then technique, which is done in increments. It consists of running for 2–2½ km, and then there is defence. There are hurdle exercises, jumping and other different types of exercises. Then there are body weight exercises. In the gym, too, there are different exercises for different ranges.

In strength training, the main focus is on weight training. Then there is weight training for core and power strengthening. Then I go for breakfast and have fruits and eggs, etc. Between 2 and 4 p.m. it is time for recovery. Also for bonding with friends and playing some games to relax. In the evening, our training session resumes once again from 4.

This is the rotational throw.

What technique is to be used depends on the fitness of the person. Besides, you also have to be focused, because, for a very short length of time, the 'work' is done for only a couple of rounds, not more than that. Whatever has to be done has to be done in this time frame.

B.S.: So, O.P. continues to range around 20 m or so. The target we have this year is also between 20 and 20½ m.

O.P.K.: Now I have just one ambition—to play at any cost. I only want to keep putting balls at a distance. What I mean is that I want to be the world's best shot-put player.

V.S.: Tell me about your life outside the sport.

O.P.K.: My village is in Haryana, near Sohna. Lakhwas is the name of my village. My father was in the army and was not at home most of the time. Ours was a joint family and there were a lot of cows and bullocks.

V.S.: Have you ever milked cows?

O.P.K.: I enjoy drinking milk. But I was never allowed to milk our cows because I was the youngest in the house. Ours was a joint family and I had many elder brothers. They were always first in things which we usually learn at home. I was at the top of the list in being mischievous.

V.S.: So, did any incident take place in school when the teacher scolded you, or was there any subject that you did not like at all?

O.P.K.: No, I never had any problem as such. All I wanted was to go and play something or get into some mischief, some prank...because my body was growing at a very fast rate and the energy levels were much higher than others. Just for enjoyment, tease somebody. The elders would give me a good thrashing (laughs).

V.S.: Since when has your height been what it is now?

O.P.K.: Since Class IX my height has been the same.

V.S.: So, this has been your height since Class IX?

O.P.K.: Yes, I have maintained that height ever since then.

V.S.: You mean to say that you will grow some more (laughs)?!

O.P.K.: Now, that seems difficult (laughs back)!

V.S.: Tell me, during your youth was there someone who spent time with you or spotted your talent?

O.P.K.: Sir, my first teacher is my mother. In the atmosphere in which I grew up, ladies are second-class citizens, and not much importance is given to them. But she was a person who nurtured a desire to do something. She wanted to prove herself. In our society in Haryana, it is a very ordinary life for any woman. She was married, and was sent to her in-laws' to be a housewife. After that I was born, and when I was growing up, I recognized a strength within her. She would be after my life to pursue a sport and wanted me to focus on that sport only. She did not allow me to play any other sport. Actually it was her own unfulfilled dreams that were coming to the fore. What she could not do, she wanted me to accomplish that. Later, when I grew up and became a little more mature, it became clear that there could be no bigger motivating force than my mother. Even now, when I am tired and have failed, I sit down and remember my mother.

V.S.: As is rightly said, there can be no comparison to a mother. No other person can think of your welfare as much or do as much as a mother can.

No matter how many responsibilities come your way, there always is the pressure from the family that you have to play well and bring home a medal...

O.P.K.: I have been lucky in every way. Perhaps that is why I have been able to continue playing. Fate has dealt out such cards to me that in every situation I have been able to play. My wife's name is Vinita and she is of such a sweet nature. In the past 4–4½ years that we have been married...

V.S.: Better be precise about that...4 or 4½ years? She will be angry... (laughs)

O.P.K.: (laughs) In the 4½ years that we have been married, with great difficulty I have managed to spend 40–50 days with her, from then till now.

V.S.: You mean in these 4 to 5 years?

O.P.K.: Yes, in all this time. She was so sporting that she did not make any demands. Without the support of the family, it is impossible to continue in this sport.

V.S.: Now, tell me something—like in my family nobody other than me plays cricket or any kind of sports. Does anybody play any kind of sports in your family?

O.P.K.: My father was in the army and there he would do some boxing and even wrestling, and tracks as well. He had some knowledge of sports, and when I began to play, he never stopped me from doing anything. He always said, 'If you want to be a sportsman, be a good one.'

V.S.: Who can talk about O.P. better than his father? Let us come to know O.P. through the eyes of his father.

So, is O.P. 'Chhotu' or 'Munna' to you (smiles)?

O.P.'s Father: He is definitely 'Munna'. Sir, it's the dream of every parent to have a son like him. The honour and accolades that he has brought us...I am sure all parents wish to have a son like him.

V.S.: When O.P. was starting out with the game, what were the initial hiccups? Tell us something about the problems and impediments that came his way.

O.P.'s Father: Initially there was a problem—no good coaches were available, and they lacked the necessary knowledge. If a good coach was found, then finding a playground was a problem. Neither did I have any resources anywhere, nor a lot of money.

V.S.: You were in the army and served the country and the army for 24 years. Today O.P. too is serving the country in a different manner. What is your opinion about this?

O.P.'s father: First of all, my hope is that he comes home with an Olympic medal. And more than that he should do something that should leave an indelible mark in his life. I understand that it's difficult to get medals, but more than the medals, it is what you have done in your life that counts. Medals can be won by many, but I want him to do something outstanding.

V.S.: The way O.P.'s father thinks is one step ahead. The wish for his son winning a medal is there, but he hopes for something even more remarkable. He should train youngsters so that India can be proud of them in the future. I salute him and his way of thinking.

O.P.K.: My entire life is focused only on sports, and within sports, on shot-put. If I win in that, my life continues smoothly. If I lose, it is equivalent to death for me. Shot-put gives me a great deal of satisfaction, which I crave internally.

V.S.: Did the experience of the London Olympics do you any good?

O.P.K.: I noted that the Olympics was a different stage altogether. Prior to that, I had never performed before a crowd of one lakh people, with all of them shouting. Nothing could be heard. It felt like I was not able to hear my own voice. However, I feel that this is the kind of stage where I can perform and be the best.

V.S.: Like when I played first-class cricket and then international cricket; in first-class cricket it was an empty ground, and in international cricket it was in front of a crowd of 50,000 people. While taking the first step, there is a little sense of fright that makes one think—where have I come, why have I come here, or am I at the wrong place? That probably happens to every player, but it happens only once, and is a one-time experience. Then the fright just goes away and you get used to it.

How much is your federation supporting you?

O.P.K.: The federation and the ministry (pauses). Sir, it seems to me that even when they want to help, they are not able to. This is simply because there is an utter lack of information regarding the sports or how a particular player has come up. The people who are at the helm are cut away from reality which the athlete has to face. That is why our players who try to go overseas have to perform well within a very short time frame. We are expected to be at the level of Olympic fitness and performance within 2–3 months of the start of practice! However, any sport is a continuous process and fitness has to be of the highest level. This is impossible in 2 or 3 months.

V.S.: Another very important fact has emerged. In countries abroad, practice is undertaken for 8 years before any effort is made to win a gold in the Olympics. But in our country it is expected that after working on the game for 3–4 months, the winning of a gold medal will not be that difficult.

What meaning does an Olympic gold have for you, O.P.?

O.P.K.: Olympic Gold plus a world record...

V.S.: You have not forgotten the world record?!

O.P.K.: Without that, it's not complete. A gold is bound to bring you fame; fame in the sense that you will be able to prove that your country, too, can produce Olympic champions. If both come together, then all dreams are fulfilled and that is the best that can happen (big smile).

V.S.: This is what we hope for brother O.P.—that in the coming Olympics he not only wins a gold, but also breaks all records. That will be the achievement of his dreams.

When I was coming to Patiala, a continuous thought was raging through my mind that I wish to see our players in the Olympic stadium and our tricolour rising. And after meeting O.P., his coach Bhupinder Singh and his father, my hope crystallized into certainty and I somehow got the assurance that it would happen, definitely happen.

This is because bottlenecks make our Indian players even stronger. Our dreams become concrete and all our problems make us that much more powerful. Further, difficulties of every sort makes our players stronger, and they are motivated by a fire to face their trials and tribulations. Who can prevent them from performing well?

3

VINESH PHOGAT

Wrestling is considered the oldest sport in India. During the era of the Mahabharata and the Ramayana it was known as 'Mull Yudh'—the local name at the time. Bali, Sugriv, Bhim and Duryodhan were all great players of the game. Through gradual stages, this game changed and took its present form of wrestling. India has given some of the best wrestlers to the world, and the biggest contribution has come from the state of Haryana. Wrestling runs in the blood of the people of Haryana. In this context the most renowned family is the Phogat family. Made up of six sisters, the Phogat family, headed by Mahavir Phogat, has changed the image of women wrestlers and wrestling in the country. And from this family of women wrestlers there is one more champion wrestler, Vinesh Phogat.

Virender Sehwag: Phogat—this has become a kind of brand name in wrestling. How do you feel about bearing this surname?

Vinesh Phogat: It feels good, sir. To make an impression and a name for oneself is very difficult. Now that it has been done, it feels very good.

V.S.: The pressures that come along with the name—how do you handle it?

V.P.: It is very difficult to keep up with the name—there is a fresh challenge each and every single day. Earlier it was to be a good wrestler. Now the expectations have gone higher and people are looking for or demanding a gold medal in the Olympics. That desire has also become instilled in me—the pressure is tremendous.

V.S.: For a player, the pressure is always more when one is practising. What happens when you are on the mat?

V.P.: Honestly, on the mat I cannot see anything but the opponent. Others say that there is always a lot of noise from the crowd, but I don't hear anything. The only thing in front of me is the opponent and all I can think about is to defeat her. Now there is no pressure—whenever I go to the mat, I try to give my 100 per cent. All I want is to win.

V.S.: This is what Sachin Tendulkar, and, in fact, Rahul Dravid, had once told me—there comes a time when they enter a zone where they can see nothing but the ball; there are no other players, no public, no side screen. I have never been to such a zone, but Vinesh goes to such a zone each time. That is why perhaps we can hope that she will bring home an Olympic medal, a gold medal.

The movie *Dangal* popularized these lines—*Maari chhoriya chhoro se kam hain ke?* (Are our girls any less than boys?) Tell me, Vinesh, how has life changed after the *Dangal* movie?

V.P.: After the movie *Dangal* I have tried to remain as private as I can be. There is already so much pressure with regard to the Olympics! To make sure that people do not add to the pressure which is already there, I try to keep myself safe by keeping a distance from them. People now know the Phogat sisters and they want to know more; they are more curious. Hence I try and keep a little distance and concentrate on my game.

V.S.: At what age did you feel that you ought to take up wrestling professionally?

V.P.: The first time I won a gold was in the Asian Championship. I was not expecting gold, but somehow I won it (laughing). All that I had wanted was to win. After that I went home and my people in the village had arranged for a grand reception for me—I was given a hero's welcome. Then I thought to myself—this is really good; they are taking photos with me, thinking, after all she has won the gold... When the women of the village came home, they would ask my mother, 'Where is Vinesh, the girl who has brought home a gold medal?' Then I thought to myself, there must be something in this, after all. I have to win; the world only recognizes you if you have done something or succeeded. At that time, I was only 14 years old.

V.S.: You were 14 years old and brought home a gold!

V.P.: Yes.

V.S.: At that age, kids do not even know what they are going to do, and you brought home a gold!

V.P.: Sir, there was a great deal of pressure from the folks at home; so the medal came. At that time I did not even think about doing well in wrestling. During those days my focus was on studies; of studying further. There were times when I was late for training after school got over, and I remember Tau ji scolding me for that (smiles). He would say, 'Stop her school; it is distracting her.' But I would insist, 'I want to go to school...' My mother ensured, on the sly, that I got to attend school, and that was also the time that I was saved from training in wrestling (laughs).

V.S.: What was so special about wrestling that you decided to take it up? Or was it that since all your sisters were opting for it, you also decided to do the same?

V.P.: When Gita–Babita had gone to play the school nationals for the first time, I was fascinated by their uniforms! I would look at them and I would say—I also want to wear the same wrestling uniform and shoes. At home there was no mat, and I so wanted to see how a mat looked, how it felt. I only wanted the experience of dressing like my sisters and playing on the mat once. That's it (smiles).

V.S.: No wrestling or anything—just to get to the mat!

V.P.: To touch the mat and see what it felt like...

V.S.: Gita and Babita must have been an inspiration—the manner in which they came to have an interest in wrestling and won medals; you must have thought to yourself that you too should bring back medals like them?

V.P.: When they brought home medals, that was when the thought struck—yes, there must be something; whenever anybody came home, they would ask, 'Gita, Babita, where are they?' That would make me angry. What was the matter with them? I was also there. Had I gone away or died or what? Were Gita and Babita the only ones in the house? With Gita and Babita, it was like this—they would have to go and win. But for me it was...I will have to go and do better than them. I would have to emerge from their towering personalities and shadows and make a name for my own self. In one way or another, it was very difficult.

V.S.: Your uncle, Mahavir Phogat, what role does he play in your life?

V.P.: He plays a great role when it comes to wrestling. If he had not supported me, who knows what turn life would have taken? There will always be huge respect for him in my heart. He taught me wrestling and I feel that wrestling has given me some of the best moments of my life. What he has instilled in me will always remain in my heart. Perhaps that day when he decided that I should also be a wrestler, God himself was inside him (getting emotional).

V.S.: What kind of a coach is Mahavir Phogat ji? Is he soft or hard?

V.P.: Very hard (laughs). I don't remember seeing him soft ever. Babita always says, no, my father is very soft. But I have never seen him in this light. Never has he said, 'Okay, okay, take a bit of rest today,' or gotten emotional. No, never. That is not him. I have always seen him angry and with bloodshot eyes.

V.S.: So how is he when he is training you? What kind of training is it?

V.P.: His training is extremely tough. He tells us to keep practising and not stop. If you stop midway or fall short of his expectations, he will hit you with a baton! I have been at the receiving end of his physical punishments so many times. I remember I used to tell my mother—what kind of a life is this? I am training hard but also getting beaten up for even small mistakes. Who behaves like this? But then, mother was helpless.

V.S.: Did you never want to leave wrestling, or leave home and go away?

V.P.: Oh yes, yes. So many times! I would tell my mother, 'What kind of game is this, wrestling? Fighting all the time? My ears have been injured...how do I look?' But then, once again, mother would say, 'Come on, child, go on trying, go on trying.'

V.S.: You lost your father at a very young age. At that time, what went through your mind?

V.P.: I was very close to my mother and never used to leave her side. I was always under her protective gaze. I would accompany my mother everywhere. I was not that close to my father, but he was, to me. When my father died, it did not have much of an impact on me; yes, I would look at my mother, and seeing her crying, would gauge that something bad had happened in the family, something was missing. But now I miss my father sometimes (with teary eyes). I was a great favourite of my father and he would always say, 'Watch out, one day my daughter will shine and fly away in a plane and I will look up to her from the ground (still crying)...

V.S.: You mentioned that you were very close to your mother and would always hang around her. What contribution did she make to your upbringing?

V.P.: Mummy has struggled a great deal. She had only two hours to rest at night. But she continued to do what she could for her children. I only had to work for gold in the Olympics and for that, three hours in the morning and three hours at night was enough. The rest of the time I could rest. But my mummy worked tirelessly, day and night. And so, whenever I am tired, fatigued or feeling down and out, two images motivate me. One is that of my mother, working hard, and the other is the Olympic gold medal. And I carry on (smiles).

V.S.: No one can ever forget the contribution of a mother. No matter how much one talks about one's mother, it is not enough. Only a mother can understand the pain of a son or a daughter. Perhaps this is the opportunity for us, players, to thank our mothers and remember them (gets emotional).

And now let's have some fun. If Vinesh has the tricks of wrestling up her sleeve, then I, too, know about having fun. This will be a rapid-fire round with Vinesh, and the game is called Viru-Pachhad.

The contestant is right in front of me—Vinesh Phogat. Ready?

Dangal or *Sultan*?

V.P.: (a pause, and then with a smile) *Dangal*!

V.S.: Aamir's body in *Dangal* or Salman's body in *Sultan*?

V.P.: Aamir Khan.

V.S.: Who is your favourite actor?

V.P.: Salman Khan.

V.S.: What is your favourite song?

V.P.: *Zindagi ek safar hai suhana, yahan kal kya ho kisne jaana* (Life is a beautiful journey, who knows what will happen tomorrow).

V.S.: That's great! By Kishore Kumar.

V.P.: Yes, sir.

V.S.: You are very fond of old Hindi numbers?

V.P.: Very much, sir.

V.S.: As a child, do you remember any incident or anecdote that left an impression on you?

V.P.: In school I used to beat up the boys in class and then get them thrashed by teachers as well by saying that they had misbehaved with me (laughing).

V.S.: You lied?

V.P.: Yes, a lot!

V.S.: If you had to go on a date, whom would you choose—an actor or a wrestler?

V.P.: A wrestler!

V.S.: Is there any particular name that you would like to bring up?

V.P.: No... (peals of laughter)

V.S.: When you go shopping, what do you buy the most?

V.P.: Hairpins...the most!

V.S.: What is your favourite food?

V.P.: Churma.

V.S.: Do you know how to cook?

V.P.: Yes, very well!

V.S.: I don't believe this.

V.P.: I am from Haryana, sir. You will have to come with me to my place to believe in my cooking skills (laughs).

V.S.: According to you, in your career, what has been your greatest realization, the greatest achievement?

V.P.: In the Commonwealth Games, when I won the gold, that was a turning point in my career. Prior to that there was no certainty about what would happen—the only thing I knew was that I had to do well. But after winning that gold, my dreams became bigger. The desire to bring gold in Olympics is so strong that it is the core of my life now.

V.S.: After qualifying for the Rio Olympics in 2016, what did you feel?

V.P.: That was a stage in my life when I was always very angry. I was angry at people who looked down upon me. I wanted to prove something to the world, and so, when I qualified for the Rio Olympics, I burst into tears. Sakshi had also qualified, and both of us, wrestlers, held each other and cried our hearts out (big smile). There was a lot of pressure since it was the last round, and we were very anxious. What if we don't qualify? How will I go back home? What will I tell my people? But then I qualified (sigh). Then when I called my mother and told her that I had qualified, she was so happy that her daughter was going to the Olympics.

V.S.: In the Olympics 2016, your famous sisters did not participate. Being part of the Phogat family, was there any kind of pressure on you?

V.P.: There was a lot of pressure on me, sir (smiles). Vinesh is a Phogat sister, and the expectations of the people, that I will bring home a medal is always there. Whenever people met me, they would comment, 'You are definitely going to bring home a medal. Somehow the feeling that I could not let them down was always there. I had to show them how hard I could work.'

V.S.: At the time of your first fight in the Olympics, what were your feelings like?

V.P.: I thought that whoever was my competitor that day would be finished. I thought, 'Today is my day and nobody can take it from me.'

V.S.: I can connect this with my own life. Something exactly like this happened with me when I stepped on to the pitch in Chennai, against South Africa. I told myself, 'Today is my day, and if it is my day, the South African team will have to pay.' I made 300 runs at the time. Perhaps it was a similar kind of day for Vinesh when she first participated in the Olympics.

In Rio, everybody had Sakshi and you on their minds. So, how did both of you boost each other's morale?

V.P.: We knew that we would definitely get a medal. But it was anybody's guess who would get what. I remember, after the weight check, when Sakshi and I came to our room, God knows why we started talking... We were telling each other, 'Look, buddy, we are getting a medal for sure. It's just that whosoever is not getting the medal, we can only imagine how she will feel (smiles). Then I suffered a slight injury and Sakshi had a slight advantage.

V.S.: In the quarter-finals, when you, unfortunately, suffered an injury, what did it feel like?

V.P.: Everything just turned blank. I could not make out where I was and why. I tried moving, but it was impossible to move any part of my body. My coach came to me and asked me to get up. I gestured and indicated to him that it was impossible for me to get up. I could see everything around me, but felt helpless. But when I was brought inside, I could feel that I had been taken off the mat. I began howling and crying and begged them to give me more and more injections so that I could get back on the mat. My physio came running, and told me that my competitor had been declared the winner. I snapped and retorted, 'How can she be declared the winner? Have I lost?' I continued in this manner for two to three hours. It was very bad.

V.S.: When there is an injury like this that pushes the player away from the mat for 5–6 months, what does it feel like?

V.P.: You become acutely aware of the importance of

wrestling in your life. In these 5–6 months I realized what place wrestling occupies in my life—how it is intertwined with my existence. Mentally, it affected me a lot. Many times I thought of giving up—it seemed everything was over. I thought, 'What do I do?' Because everybody forgets you. At such a time nobody asks for you. To control oneself and also continue with the training—that is very challenging.

V.S.: How was the time of recovery? How did you handle yourself at that time? What did you do?

V.P.: When the operation was going on, even before the operation, I told the surgeon, sir, if you insist on an operation, then I want to be better than before. If I am going to be beaten and taken away from the mat, please do not operate. I would rather leave wrestling. The surgeon had assured me that I would do well after the operation. And then it was in my post-operative period that I found real motivation. My team at JSW made a remarkable contribution in my comeback. They would always tell me to remain positive; they would encourage me by saying that I had a rock-solid resolve and that I should remain like that. They were like friends, and it helped me a lot in my recovery. The positive vibes were there. If it would not have been for them, I think I would never have been able to make a comeback or stay on the mat.

V.S.: Let me tell you something. In 2008, after I suffered my first injury, which was in the shoulder, I made my second double century. It is always good after an injury.

V.P.: After that, sir, the rage was so overwhelming, I felt like I would chew up anyone who confronted me!

V.S.: I am seated here in Lucknow, in the premises of the Sports Authority of India. All the wrestlers here are working very hard. There is someone who is working just as hard as them. He is an ex-Olympian, the winner of the Dhyan Chand Award, chief wrestling coach Kuldeep Malik. How and where did you come across Vinesh Phogat?

KULDEEP MALIK: I met Vinesh in 2013, when the girl came here to this camp for the first time to join the junior team...and then later I kept track of her in the senior team. When I saw her speed...it was excellent! I could depend on her. No matter how tough a task I would give her, she would do it.

V.S.: The injuries sustained during the Olympics, how serious were they and how long did they take to heal?

K.M.: It takes one year to heal up to 95 per cent. I am leaving that 5 per cent out because as a player even you know that there is some degree of hesitation.

V.S.: There is some degree of hesitation and there surely is some pain. Every player learns to play with some degree of pain. Pain becomes a part of a player's life. So, now that she is back on the mat and is also training and wrestling, what do you feel?

K.M.: Once again, the same hopes that were there in 2016 are arising—no matter what happens, she will surely bring back a medal.

V.S.: From the point of view of a coach, what strength does Vinesh possess?

K.M.: It is a blessing that God has given her such a body... such a structure! She has a natural power.

V.S.: What is her weakness?

K.M.: We don't talk about the weaknesses of our players (laughs). We are working on them, if any (smiles).

V.S.: Well said, Kuldeep ji...the sign of a good coach is that he never talks about his protégé's weakness. He looks at it, observes it and tries and removes that weak spot, and that's what Kuldeep ji is doing with Vinesh.

K.M.: Vinesh is such a wrestler that as a coach you have to be very careful while coaching her.

V.P.: I take a lot of risks and am never afraid of doing something out of the box. My body structure is very good, and if I am attacked, points will be given only with a great deal of difficulty.

K.M.: Her mode of attacking is very good and noteworthy. If she makes a direct attack, then it is impossible to withstand it.

V.P.: Coach ji has a plan, a schedule about how to proceed. Since the competition is drawing near, we practise on the grounds in the morning. On Mondays, in the evening, we do mat training for three hours. On Tuesdays, we do mat training twice, but then that is slightly different from usual. Less attention is paid to technique, and there are bouts— matches—the sort that are done in competitions. This is so that we get into the habit of fighting. On Wednesday, we have gym training or free weight training. This is done according to a plan—whether it is a competition or not. On Thursday, in the morning, it is on the grounds, and in the evening, on the mat. On Friday, it is once again matches, actual matches that take place. On Saturday, it is long distance, cross country— anything between 6–10 km. It is to boost stamina. Speed is very important, and so that is what I focus on, to boost it.

K.M.: The mental strength of this girl is so great that there is no one else in comparison. I am of the opinion that in whatever competition she participates, even in the Olympics, she will definitely win a medal.

V.P.: I want to carve a niche and make a name for myself, so that if any reference is made to the sports, then, just the way Sushil pehelwan ji has made a name for himself, I want my name to be taken alongside his. In women's wrestling, it should be Vinesh Phogat and only Vinesh Phogat.

V.S.: For any sportsperson, what is most upsetting is returning from the arena without playing. Vinesh has seen that and crossed that hurdle. Now she is ready for a bright future and she has all our good wishes with her. There is no doubt in my mind that she will live up to all our expectations. All the best, Vinesh. Jai Hind!

4

SUYASH JADHAV

I am very excited because the person I am going to meet today is a true Olympian, Suyash Jhadav. The motto of the Olympics is faster, higher, stronger. Suyash, too, believes in it. He thinks fast, has lofty ideals and is determined. In the Olympics, more than the actual winning, it is the participation that is important. For Suyash, too, whether, he wins or not is not important—what matters to him is how much he has laboured. Suyash Jadhav is a Paralympics swimmer, having lost both his arms.

Virender Sehwag: So, who motivated you to start swimming and made you believe that you could think of taking up this sport as a profession?

Suyash Jadhav: My father was a national-level swimmer. He wanted me to achieve what he had not been able to. So, with that end in mind, he taught me swimming when I was three years old. At the time he taught me swimming, he also started my formal training. Thus, it was my father who used to inspire me; it was he who was my first coach. It was he who told me that I would have to learn swimming, I would have to become a champion. That's it—he was everything for me.

V.S.: Tell me about the incident that was responsible for changing your life completely.

S.J.: When I was in Class VI, I think it was in 2004...there was a wedding of a cousin scheduled in a school premises. One day before the wedding, I had gone to school to play. There were a lot of electric wires; you know those steel rods used for construction? I held on to one and tried to balance myself. Since I could not hold my balance, I raised the other hand to hold on to it. That too got stuck to it. Both my hands got electrified. I was in the hospital for almost a year. But it was of no use, as I lost both my hands. At that time I thought that I would never be able to swim again, and all the dreams of my father would end. The entire family was greatly disturbed and did not know how I would carry on in the future.

V.S.: After this, in what manner did your life change and what difficulties came your way?

S.J.: I was very young at the time and for every little thing I needed my mother's help. There were no major problems as such. But gradually, as I began to grow up, I realized that if I asked my family members for help in each and every matter, I would become totally dependent on them. There were times when I felt depressed, and sometimes I wished for my hands. I would watch the kids play cricket...and I loved that game. I would feel very bad when I saw them playing.

V.S.: Suyash Jhadav has undergone so much in life. I decided to speak with his parents because they also had to deal with this tragedy.

Mr Jadhav: All the children of his age would have fun and jump about, but my son could neither have fun, nor play; it hurt me greatly.

Mrs Jadhav: We were very troubled. We did not know what he would do and how.

Mr Jadhav: The doctors had said, 'Don't worry, he will be able to do everything.' His primary problem was to put on clothes! His biggest challenge was how to button his shirts. So we decided to do away with shirts having buttons and bought T-shirts for him instead. Similarly, trousers gave way to loose track pants. These were our small efforts, but they were really big for him (smiles with tears in his eyes).

At home we don't discriminate. I have told him that you will live like normal people do. We will try and not over-protect you (smiles). In the house, we live together like a normal happy family (smiles again).

V.S.: Suyash could have led a comfortable life with his parents. Despite not being independent, his parents would have taken care of him. But that was not his choice, and he felt that he should be independent and also become a role model for others...show them that despite having no hands, he could play sports and be regarded as no less than anybody else.

Suyash, what has happened has happened. Now it is time to move forward. Where did this inspiration come from?

S.J.: My father said, do not look back on what has happened. It is better to focus on what you have. What do I have? I have a certain skill—I can swim very well. So, don't keep thinking about what you don't have; work with what you have. Success will definitely be yours.

V.S: Excellent! But when you began swimming for the second time, after so many years, how much did your parents support you?

S.J.: Even they did not know whether I would be able to swim. There is a certain religious place where my entire family goes—all were swimming in a pond there. My father felt that I could also join in; he encouraged me to give it a shot. He assured me that they all were there, so he could jump in the pond if I needed help. I jumped into the water.

That was the first time I entered any kind of water body since the accident. I realized I was able to swim. My father again became hopeful. It was my father who was my greatest support. My neighbours and relatives would always discourage my father, telling him not to go ahead with this. Of course, they spoke out of concern, advising my father against putting pressure on me to swim. But my father was adamant.

Mr Jadhav: I was sure that in the days to come he was bound to do well. It didn't matter that he had lost both his hands. He would swim, and swim well! I knew this. Further, I told him, whether or not you want to go ahead with this, you must never leave exercising or forget the spirit of competition. You are a good swimmer and you have to do well (smiles).

Mrs Jadhav: In his peace lies our peace. If my son is happy, we, too, are happy.

Mr Jadhav: In the village, I trained him first. Even if he is alone, he is very strong. He has never indulged in self-pity—never thought, 'Oh, I am physically disabled and I am a swimmer...how can I do all this by myself?' He is an extremely positive person. Negativity is not one of his traits.

V.S.: Suyash, your father was your first coach. For how long did he coach you?

S.J.: My father taught me swimming when I was just three years old. He made the basic tenets of swimming clear at that time itself; like, there are strokes such as backstroke, butterfly, breaststroke and freestyle. He taught me all of them.

V.S.: Did you ever make any excuses, like breaking the routine from Monday to Saturday by saying things like, 'I am not in the mood today' or 'I have body ache'...something like that?

S.J.: (laughs) I remember an anecdote. I was in Bangalore for training, and timings there are very different from where I come from. I was used to late mornings like 7–9 or 8–10, but in Bangalore they expect you to get up at 4 in the morning and be in the pool by 5. If you are late even by 5 minutes, they will not allow you to enter the pool. So initially it was very tough for me (laughs). I used to think, 'Oh! I should let it go and sleep for some time.' But then I always used to get up and be in the pool by 5 a.m. (smiles).

V.S.: Like all other youngsters, Suyash thought of these excuses, but he did not really implement them. Even sportspersons such as cricketers like us think of innumerable excuses sometimes and miss major practices. If I talk about myself, I would suddenly develop make-belief fever that would last as long as the practice would continue. After that I would just get up and go and play in the match. We cricketers make many such excuses. Even while in the cricket team we made excuses. If we had to go for practice around 8 or 9 and did not feel like it, we called the physio and falsely complained about some pain, such as a stomach ache, pain in the back, etc. Suyash also must have thought about making such excuses, but he never really implemented them, and the result is for all to see (smiles). Perhaps that is why he is our hope in the Paralympics.

Who told you all about the Paralympics?

S.J.: After losing my hands in the accident, two or three years went by just like that. In the meanwhile, father was exploring where Para Championships are held, and the possibility of my participation. One of my father's friends, we call him Umesh sir, has been a para swimmer, and used to participate in such events. It was he who said there were Paralympic competitions in swimming. I came to know about the Paralympics then, as he told me all about it.

V.S.: What is the best advice your father gave you?

S.J.: To continue to be patient. At a time when nothing seems to be working out, just continue to be patient and go on doing what you are doing. Just wait for times to get better.

V.S.: From your first international tournaments till 2016 in Rio, how has your journey been? Tell us something about that.

S.J.: Actually, it was from 2007 that I began swimming. The first international competition was in 2009. From 2007–2016,

I won 90+ medals. My best achievement has been going to Russia in 2015 and qualifying for the Olympics. In 2013 itself I had visualised standing on the Olympic podium. So from that time I was working and practising very hard. When I qualified and went to Rio, the dream had begun to feel real. We generally watch the Olympics on the television screen, but going there and experiencing that atmosphere... I was getting a chance to compete with all the top athletes, and I was able to actually stay there—it felt amazing!

V.S: When you returned to India from Rio, there was a message on your mobile—from the Prime Minister. Would you tell us something about that?

S.J.: As we were returning, and when we were in Amsterdam for a layover, some of the athletes had no charge on their phones, and some had other issues like it always is when your phone is on international roaming. I was the first one to switch on my mobile and connect it to the WiFi...and to my amazement I saw a message from the Prime Minister's Office. All the Paralympic participants were invited to meet the Prime Minister on the 24th of that month. I could hardly believe my eyes! I was elated beyond words; it meant so much to us. We could not believe that our Prime Minister wanted to meet us (teary-eyed).

V.S.: You all have deserved this. Our Prime Minister was very happy on hearing the news of the success of our Paralympians at the event (smiles).

Tell me something, in order to accomplish your goals, what do you do?

S.J.: In order to achieve my goals, most of all I focus on my training. After that, consistency. Whatever I do for my training, I do it with consistency. That is to say, I never miss any session.

V.S.: What appears a challenge to us is merely daily routine for Suyash. Starting with getting up in the morning and reaching the swimming pool, his day passes in much the same manner as an average athlete's.

S.J.: My swimming begins at 5 in the morning. The morning training session focuses on stroke techniques. Then from 10–12.30 it is time for the gym session. In swimming, we focus mainly on the upper part of the body which is used the most. I have a problem with my hands, and so there is not too much concentration on the upper body. No matter how much I concentrate on the upper body pull workout, it won't be of much use. But yes, if I do the lower body pull exercises, it is useful to me.

We also met the person who has trained Suyash professionally. His name is Abhijit Garg, and he says...

Abhijit Garg: Normal swimmers use their hands more. It's the reverse with Suyash for obvious reasons. He uses his legs more. It is necessary to make his legs stronger.

S.J.: Once the gym session is over, the attention is shifted to core training, which is most important for swimming. I go home and rest. Lunch is at 1.30 p.m. In the evening, we work mostly on speed. My main stroke is 50 m butterfly. My technique is a little off there and so I am trying to rectify it. I also pay attention to the breathing pattern and kicking.

A.G.: The Olympics is in 2020. By then there will be so much improvement in him that he will be able to beat his own time.

S.J.: My biggest competitor is my own timing. In order to get this, for the 50 m butterfly, I must make 28 seconds and for the 50 m freestyle I need 27 seconds. In the Paralympics, I will win a medal in 2020 and my dream is to set my own record in 2024.

V.S: If I ask you who is your idol, from whom do you get inspiration, whose name would you take?

S.J.: My idol is Michael Phelps. Whenever I see his clips on YouTube, when I see his practice sessions or stroke techniques, I feel very good. Watching him is very inspiring. I imagine myself in his place—like if he is doing something, I can do it too...and I imagine the results. That is to say that I keep comparing myself to him (smiles).

V.S: You are also very active on social media. You have started Swimmer Sunday Initiative. What is this all about?

S.J.: As the name suggests, it takes place on Sundays. We record the practice and swimming sessions to know what swimming is all about. It is then posted on Facebook on Sunday so that people like me who are aspiring swimmers know how it is done, and most importantly, how their goals can be achieved. I want to inspire and motivate physically disabled swimmers so that they can join me in swimming after seeing these videos. They should be motivated and inspired— that's the idea. If I can achieve this, inspire and motivate more such swimmers, India will have greater chances of winning a medal. Under any circumstance, I have to win in the Olympics, bring back a medal and break records. Till I achieve that, I am not going to stop.

Secondly, I want to build an academy of my own, somewhat like the Deccan Gymkhana, which is supporting me in what I am doing now, so that talented swimmers and athletes can come and join and train there. I want to build a campus for them so that they can concentrate on their sports completely. I don't know whether I will be successful or not, but it is a dream I have.

V.S.: It is only if we dream that these goals can be fulfilled. My father had also dreamed of establishing Sehwag International School. He could not fulfil it, but as his son, I did. If you cannot fulfil your dream then maybe someone else will. But you can play a very vital role in taking that academy forward if you manage to do it.

The position in which Suyash is, today, has been possible because many people have supported him in this journey. And one of them is GoSports Foundation.

I went to meet the executive director of the foundation, Deepthi Bopaiah.

Deepthi, tell us something about what was the inspiration behind GoSports Foundation.

Deepthi Bopaiah: We are nine years old and started this foundation so that a talented athlete is not forced to drop out of sports. We ask the athletes to only focus on their game and we take care of everything else in their professional life.

V.S: How is GoSports Foundation helping Suyash?

D.B.: For Suyash, we are stressing on focus training. We are focusing on his nutrition plan. I think when he went to Rio, there wasn't too much focus on fitness training. That is, perhaps, lacking, and we can work on it. We are also working with a mental trainer for him; to build up his confidence, focus and help him plan better.

V.S: What is the difference between a Paralympic player and a normal Olympic player in terms of their training? What are the challenges you face?

D.B.: In our opinion, there is no difference. But, there are many challenges because as far as the physique is concerned, it is difficult for a Paralympic athlete to be like others. So we need to create that support system. But one thing we have learned about differently-abled people is that they don't give excuses. Unlike us, who complain regularly about aching legs, headaches, shoulder pain etc., they don't give any excuses. They are out there struggling, fighting their physical limitations and going all the way.

V.S.: Today I would like to wish Suyash all the very best for the next Paralympics. But before that, on behalf of my country and myself, I would like to thank him. Thank you, Suyash, for teaching us a new definition of positivity. Thank you for inspiring us and being our role model. Thank you for teaching us the strength of self-confidence. Thank you Suyash for telling us that life is not a problem, but a solution. Here's wishing Suyash all the very best before the next Paralympics. Jai Hind!

5

SAKSHI MALIK

There is nothing that our daughters cannot do—they are capable of bringing down the stars from the sky. Another such daughter of Haryana, who is a role model for budding wrestlers, an inspiration to girls and brings joy to all Indians is Sakshi Malik.

Virender Sehwag: Sakshi, tell me something—you are from Haryana, and so am I. What is the special diet that is provided to the sons and daughters of Haryana that so many wrestlers are emerging from that state?

Sakshi Malik: (smiles) Forget about the diet, sir. Even the water of Haryana has power enough to produce a wrestler. We have wells where you can still get fresh water. Pure butter and clarified butter (ghee) is available. Our forefathers have been wrestling since a very long time. So, in some way or the other, it is in our blood itself.

V.S.: In Haryana, if you compare the time when you were growing up with the present time, what differences do you observe?

S.M.: There are a lot of differences that I have noticed. Take, for example, the fact that there was only one mat, and at the maximum, only 3–4 girls could practise. We would also have to practise with men, because there was a shortage of partners, and then gradually, as wrestling became widespread in India, many more men and women began participating. Now there are thirty girls in the centre where once there were only 3–4 girls. Gita-Babita came and then gradually girls from other states began coming in. It all started from here.

V.S.: What does wrestling mean to you? What place does it have in your life?

S.M.: During Diwali, we all pray and worship God. When I first understood the game and realized how much I loved it, that Diwali I brought out my costume and wrestling shoes. All the other family members were preparing plates with sweets and all other things needed for the prayers. I brought all my wrestling things and kept them there, near the deity. My brother was stupefied and wondered what I was doing. I told him to keep quiet (laughs). Then I got some of the blessed turmeric powder and put them on my shoes and everything else. That tradition still continues. My mother applies the holy mark in all my kits. There is nothing more attractive to me than wrestling—wrestling is the most important thing in my life.

V.S.: I also know a man like this—Sachin Tendulkar. We call him the God of cricket. But even God worships God. He places his own honour at the feet of the Almighty and hopes it will be blessed by the Almighty and he carries with him this blessing, and then that all-important century is made. That is why Sachin Tendulkar is regarded as a God in the world of cricket—he has made a hundred centuries in international cricket. This is something like what Sakshi Malik is doing—placing her shoes and kit in front of the Almighty so that his blessings are there, and with that she will bring back a gold medal for India.

What or who is it in wrestling that inspires you the most, Sakshi?

S.M.: Believe me, I knew nothing about wrestling—what is the kit or mat or anything of that sort. All that I knew was that I would have to wrestle. You will not believe it, but I always wondered how a mat so big was brought inside a hall through those small doors (both laugh)! I wondered whether they first placed those big mats and then built a hall around them (more laughter). But then it was raining one day and we had to take out the mats and then I realized that the big mat is made up of small parts (smiles). The point I am trying to make is that this was my initial knowledge about the game, but equally important is the fact that I was very curious about wrestling. I liked its costume, the mats, the entire paraphernalia.

V.S.: One person who helped you a great deal?

S.M.: Dada ji. My grandfather used to wrestle, and in the village he was known as 'Pehelwan Saab'—and it fascinated me—the stories about my Dada ji, the name he was given...

V.S.: So you also want to be known as Pehelwan Sahiba (laughs).

S.M.: No, not exactly (shy and smiling), but I would hear them calling out my grandfather's name. Then one of my seniors—she was a wrestler—her picture came in the newspapers one day. I was so inspired by that image that I went to my father and requested him to let me play this sport. He took me to a nearby stadium and I began my training there.

V.S.: As a child, who inspired you the most?

S.M.: Actually, it was the aeroplane! When I began wrestling, my seniors would tell me that whosoever came first in India would get to sit on a flight and visit a foreign country, to play and participate in international events. And that became my driving force (big smile). Then, of course, later on, I understood all about competitions—about the Asian Games, Olympics etc. and then, everything fell into place.

V.S.: And ever since, you have not got down from the plane (laughs)?!

S.M.: (laughs) Yeah...sort of.

V.S.: Actually, Sakshi, I have been born and brought up in Delhi. Even my dream was to be able to sit in an aeroplane. And I got that opportunity in 1998 when I participated in the Under–19 World Cup in South Africa. It was a great feeling to be on a plane (smiles), and ever since then I have also not got down from the plane (both laugh).

S.M.: Sir, like you have seen, in Lucknow, where we train, we can see the plane at a very low height. In the morning, when we would be in the field for training, the planes would land from very close quarters. Takeoffs would also happen, and these sights would inspire me. I always used to think that one day I would be on these planes with an Olympic medal in my hand. And believe me, sir, that would give me a different kind of energy. I have now experienced that also—sitting in a plane with an Olympic medal in my hand.

V.S.: In the Rio Olympics, the entire attention was focused on Vinesh Phogat. Then, after her unfortunate injury, she had to return home. How much pressure was there on you to perform and win a medal, since all hopes were on you now?

S.M.: Actually, sir, ever since I began wrestling, Vinesh and I have been the best of friends. We have been training partners, been in competitions together, shared the same room and even during Rio we were together. We were in the same weight category, our bout was also on the same day. And both of us told each other that we would win medals. I had a feeling that if Vinesh had 90 per cent chance of getting a medal, I was also not far behind, and that I could also get a medal. People had more hopes from Vinesh since she had performed well in the Asian Games. So, during Rio, she won her first bout, and so did I. Both of us were very happy. But then the worst happened and in the second bout she was injured. I was preparing for my bout and Kuldeep sir entered, and tears were streaming down his eyes. You can imagine how much pressure I would have felt on seeing my coach like that. Kuldeep sir, with tears in his eyes, told me that Vinesh had been injured and now the only chance of winning a medal rested on me. And I was then thinking to myself, 'Come what may, I have to give my 100 per cent and get a medal. You see, wrestling competitions in the Olympics are always towards the end, and by that time India had not won any medal. So naturally all hopes were on wrestling and more so on Vinesh and myself. And now, with Vinesh gone, I was the only one left, and of course, the boys. So I had to give my 100 per cent, and I did so.

V.S.: After Sakshi won the bronze medal in the Olympics, all of you will remember one picture of her. A person had lifted Sakshi up on his shoulder—and that person was coach Kuldeep Malik. Not only did he pick Sakshi up on his shoulder, but he also shouldered all of Sakshi's responsibility, right up to Rio.

And so it is time now to meet Kuldeep Malik.

V.S.: When and where did you first meet Sakshi Malik?

Kuldeep Malik: Sakshi had come to the camp for the first time in 2011. When she was at the junior level in the Patiala camp, I had seen the girl and she had seemed to be a nice and talented girl. I had seen her focus and right attitude towards practice even in the year 2011.

V.S.: Do you want to share any interesting anecdote from the time when you were training Sakshi?

K.M.: We were playing handball one day and Sakshi hit the competitor who was also a wrestler with such force that she fell a few metres away and hit a mango tree (both laugh). I told Sakshi that if she had hit this girl with such a force in wrestling she might not have survived! I then trained her how to attack, how to utilize her force and energy, showed her how to attack on the legs. She has a way of attacking on the legs—that's her style, and it is unique. The Almighty has given her such a body and power to attack. Initially, her weakness was that she was not that strong psychologically, but now she has overcome that weakness also.

V.S.: When the medal was won in the Rio Olympics, we all celebrated so much back in India. All of us went berserk with happiness. In the last round, when the fight ended, what were your feelings?

K.M.: I had never felt so happy in my life. Somehow, and I don't know why, it did not feel like Sakshi had won the medal; it felt like my country had won the medal. That day was a day of victory for my country. Even more than Sakshi, it was my country's victory. It was for India...

V.S.: You are right, Kuldeep ji. Even we felt the same way, that this is not Sakshi's medal, but a medal for the whole of India, the entire country had won.

So, Kuldeep ji, after the success of Rio 2016, what changes have you seen in Sakshi? What are the improvements you want Sakshi to make, so that she can get gold instead of bronze?

K.M.: I have seen very few players who change that much, and that too, in such a positive manner as Sakshi has done. In practice or even during training, she is more intense, more disciplined. Rio has made her even stronger.

V.S.: What are your plans for Sakshi in the future?

K.M.: I tell Sakshi only this. You have won a medal, which is very good. You must also remain a good person. You should concentrate on 2020 Olympics, and whenever you have any doubt, just try and address it.

We now move to the intense training and practice session

and see for ourselves how Sakshi trains and what her regime is like.

S.M.: I was twelve years old when I began wrestling. Since then, I haven't known what weekends are! I don't go for movies either. I have to train both times of the day, and if, by any chance, I am hanging out with friends even for some time during the day, the evening training gets affected. There are a lot of sacrifices that one has to make. There must be total focus at a certain level—it must be wrestling, and that's it. Nothing should remain on one's mind but wrestling.

V.S.: What kind of routine do you follow?

S.M.: There are different schedules for the entire week. Like, for example, on Mondays, it varies, on Tuesdays both the times it is mat training, on Wednesdays it is power session because in wrestling you need everything—speed, power, strength and stamina. But most important is working on the mat. There are techniques and tactics that you employ; it is like playing with the mental makeup of your opponent. Make her feel that you are going to attack from one side but in reality you attack from another side; surprise her with your moves. My favourite attack is the leg attack. My medal in the Olympics was also by virtue of this favourite attack.

V.S.: What kind of diet do you follow?

S.M.: Actually, our diet keeps changing right through the year, so it is not fixed. As the competition draws near, we start eating very less. There is no fat, clarified butter or sweet in our diet during this period. We have to fight with reduced weight—like my weight now is 62–63 and I fight in the 58 kg category. So if I have to play, I have to lose 5–6-kg. We do this within 7 days so that there is instant loss and instant energy gain. If we do it as a long process, the recovery will also be an equally long process. As you have also seen, we wear a sauna suit, and by that itself, we lose almost 2½ kg a day!

Let me tell you what the most difficult part of wrestling is—you know, it does not matter to me whether I am asked to practise for two hours at a stretch, three to four times a day. The most difficult part is losing weight. I remember during the last two days of the Olympics I was only sipping water so that I didn't gain even a gram of weight. They are extremely strict with weight and even if my weight is 50 gm more than what my category permits, I will not be allowed to enter the mat. They don't even give a second chance.

V.S.: At this time who is your major or greatest competitor—whom you regard as your greatest hurdle in winning?

S.M.: When I began wrestling, I would hear the names of Saori Yoshida and Icho Kaori who had won the gold medal three times consecutively. So I would think—when will I get to see them? In 2012, when I went for the Senior World Wrestling Championships for the first time, I saw these two girls from Japan training on the field—and I lost all concentration on my own training (laughing). I kept on looking at them and wondered when I could be like them... It is God's blessing and because of my dedication that in the 2016 Rio Olympics I stood on the same podium with them. It meant so much (gets emotional)...

V.S.: This happens to every sportsperson. He or she gets overawed on seeing their role models, and forgets practising! This is what happened to Sakshi Malik, and this is what happened to me when I went outside India and represented my country; when I went to South Africa, Australia or New Zealand—I saw the English or Australian team practising, and my attention was more on how they practised, rather than practising myself. But it was always there in the mind that one day or the other I would defeat them, and that is what Sakshi Malik has shown she can do.

In the Rio Olympics when you were fighting your bouts, at the last moment, before winning, you were behind the score rate—what were the thoughts going through your mind at that time?

S.M.: I had only 9 seconds and I was losing. I knew I had to fight to the end. The mind goes absolutely blank—because though I had 9 seconds, my opponent was still winning. So, how could I cover my points in 9 seconds? But then you have no choice but to attack, and I did exactly that. It was impossible to believe what happened in those 9 seconds.

V.S.: I also met some of the prominent people in wrestling to understand their views on Sakshi Malik. I first met Brij Bhushan Sharan Singh who is the president of the Wrestling Federation of India.

Brij Bhushan Singh: You just take note of this thing—that this girl has power. There is no lack of strength. This girl saved the pride of the country and wrestling as well.

Jagdish Kaliraman (former wrestler): When you go to the level of the Olympics and play five rounds, it is very important that you are physically fit; you must be mentally strong and where techniques are concerned, very adept. Each wrestler must have a strategy.

If we talk about Indian wrestlers, what the future is or what the future in the Olympics is, her future is very bright. There are many new names in the team we can talk about for freestyle women's wrestling. But the two prominent names for the 2020 Olympics which have all but been decided are Sakshi Malik and Vinesh Phogat. In my opinion, India can win 5–6 medals in the 2020 Olympics.

V.S: So what was your first reaction when you won that medal?

S.M.: My first reaction was... 'Sir, flag! Give me our flag!' Holding aloft the flag I ran around the mat—I was living my dream.

V.S.: I can relate to that feeling very well. We won the World Cup and ran around the field. Sakshi Malik, too, did the same—the most important factor that inspires us all to participate in competitions—she took the flag and sprinted around the mat. After the Rio Olympics, overnight, Sakshi Malik became an idol. So, in what ways has your life changed since then, Sakshi?

S.M.: When I returned to India after the Rio Olympics, there were a lot of changes. Sir had told me to wear clothes that could withstand crowd frenzy because people would go crazy (laughs), and they were (more laughter)! When I reached India, even more people had come to receive me. Life has changed a great deal—now people know me and shower me with love.

V.S.: A major agenda of the Haryana government, where there is a big difference in the sex ratio, is the Beti Bachao, Beti Padhao yojana. You have become the face of this programme. What prompted you to do so, and don't you think it is a huge responsibility?

S.M.: My mother also works in this sphere—and when I was made the brand ambassador for Beti Bachao, Beti Padhao, it brought me great happiness. Gradually, a difference is being brought about in Haryana. When I go to different places I tell people that girls are not inferior in any way—give them equal chances. Girls, too, can achieve a lot. That these small changes are in fact taking place in our society and I am playing a role in it is very encouraging and overwhelming.

V.S.: Each athlete dreams of bringing home the Olympic medal, and your dream has also come true. Now what is your ultimate goal?

S.M.: Goals or ambitions never come to an end. You begin to like the sport, the fame and fortune so much that you cannot even think of walking away from it. You strive to do more and more to retain it and to achieve more.

Like I was telling you, I don't have a medal in the World Championships—I have to win that. In the Commonwealth Games the silver has to be turned to gold, and the major ambition is the gold in the Olympics.

V.S.: While it is true that Sakshi Malik's dream of bringing home a medal from Rio was fulfilled, all her other dreams still remain. Thanks to all the hard work that she is putting in, the day is not very far when she will be able to turn the bronze into silver and the silver into gold. Our best wishes are with her.

So far the slogan had been Beti Bachao, Beti Padhao. But after Sakshi's success, something has to be added to the slogan. Beti Khilao. We need to encourage our daughters a little more and then we will see that the journey from Rohtak to Rio will be no big deal. I pray to the Almighty that at every step of the way Sakshi meets with great success. Jai Hind!

6

DUTEE CHAND

The racing track is the life and soul of athletes. The heartbeats of the nation can be heard in the footfall of all athletes. If one observes the tattered shoes of those running along these tracks, there are also silver and gold medals adorning them. These tracks have seen everything, the dedication and labour, the struggle and also the confidence of the athlete. A racing track accompanies both the dream and the reality of an athlete.

In my entire career in one day cricket, there have been 15 centuries; but there is this one young girl of twenty years who has made 15 national and state records for herself. Looking at her record, one can easily say that by the time she retires, she will have made 100 records for herself, like Sachin Tendulkar.

Friends, we have with us Dutee Chand.

Virender Sehwag: Will you tell all of us what meaning this sport has for you?

Dutee Chand: In my life there is nothing but sports (smiles). Sports is everything to me because I have got everything only through it. My family's background and situation also improved, and I got a lot of fame as well.

V.S.: What is the difference between you and other sprinters?

D.C.: Well, I think there is not much difference in the way we all practise. I have participated in a lot of events. Previously, I was a marathon runner; after that I came to the middle-distance genre—800 and 1500 m. From there it was 400–200. In my opinion it is very important for a sportsperson to have proper rest and proper training. I never compromised on these two factors. Since my childhood till this day I have remained away from my family to continue this training. In my life there have been 3–4 major achievements. But I am still continuing training because whatever God has sent me for, I have to do that for my country and present it to him. That is the dream that I am pursuing wholeheartedly and am moving ahead for this purpose. That, I think, is the only difference.

V.S.: Dutee ji, at the age of seventeen, you were the first female Indian to enter the IAAF. So, how did you feel?

D.C.: I felt very happy that I was the first Indian woman athlete to participate in the 100-m IAAF World Championships. I not only participated but went up till the semi-finals. It felt very good that my timing, 11.63, was a record of sorts. I was sure that if I concentrated on this, I would be able to participate in the Olympics in this category. And that dream came true when I participated in the 100-m race in the Olympics.

V.S.: What was the experience of the Rio Olympics like?

D.C.: Oh! Participating in the Rio Olympics—well, it was the first time I had participated in the Olympics, and it felt very good (sighs and smiles). I felt very happy from inside—after all, participation in the Olympics is a dream for all sportspersons. That was my dream that came true. When I went there, all the famous athletes I had heard about and seen on TV or newspapers were right there in front of me. I got an opportunity to see them from close quarters and also chat with them. Just like a fair is held in the centre of the city, Olympics seemed like a huge festival to me—people had come from every corner. I like Usain Bolt a lot and also Shelly-Ann Fraser-Pryce. Seeing them from close quarters felt very good. There were so many things I learnt from them. I followed them completely—how they did their block starting, how they used to warm up and relax. It was an exhilarating experience seeing the best and learning from them.

V.S.: Dutee ji, should I tell you something? Sachin Tendulkar is my role mode. I would watch him bat on television and would imitate his actions. I would emulate his strokes and play like him. Just by looking at his training videos on YouTube, a lot can be learnt. When you met these renowned players and noted their warm up procedures, what kind of emotions engulfed you?

D.C.: I was a little afraid—having come to participate in such an important competition. The entire country was expecting that Dutee would bring home a medal—so I was constantly thinking, 'Will I be able to fulfil this dream or not?' They were also all taller than me. If judged physically, I looked the smallest, and neither was I as muscular as the others. I prayed to the Almighty that I may get the fruits of all the labour I had put in and run to the very best of my ability.

V.S.: What problems arose? What do you think happened in Rio?

D.C.: My competition was on the 12th and I reached on the 5th. I felt that there was a great deal of climatic difference between Rio and India. Further, the competition took place at night. The Olympic Association had already notified us that the event would be at night. But I was not able to practise at night and that had its effect on my performance. The chill in the air also had an effect—my body remained cold. I did not get a chance to warm my body and neither did I have any idea how to do so. That did have some impact, and on such a massive ground, at this level, running in front of everybody, I was a bit awkward. I was somewhat nervous, and that was also a problem.

V.S.: Now, tell me, what kind of a person is your coach Ramesh ji?

D.C.: He treats all the athletes as his own children. If there is any physical problem or a disturbance within someone's family, he tries to settle these issues. I think he is a very good coach because since the time I started training under him, I made a record in the nationals in the 100-m race. Ever since then my flow of medals has continued—in India and in Asia. Coach always looks after me as his child which is unusual because usually a coach trains with you at the time of a race and then leaves. But my coach always calls me and tells me that the training will begin at such and such time and that I have to prepare my body accordingly. Then in between he also calls and asks whether I have had lunch. He looks after me in every way.

V.S.: Has he ever been angry with you or have you ever left training, or is there anything else that you would like to share with all of us?

D.C.: Whenever there is any problem with others, it is always vented on me (laughs). If he is not happy with any player's performance or fitness level, or any particular athlete has not done their training properly, he gets angry with me. He tells me, 'Are you willing to do this, or do you insist on saying—this is not possible, that is not possible?' So it's like this—he is all right with me but the moment any athlete does something wrong, the anger is directed at me (laughs).

V.S.: (laughs) Dutee, you know why he behaves like this— because he has a lot of expectations from you. He knows that you are very talented and are capable of bringing India medals. My coach also behaved in a similar manner with me. He would be upset with someone else and he would vent it on me. This is because he knew that I was a good player and had talent to perhaps play for the country. That is why he would be even more terse with me. That could also be the reason why your coach easily gets angry with you—because he knows you are talented and are capable of bringing home medals (both chuckle).

You will remember that in the Los Angeles Olympics of 1984, P.T. Usha lost the opportunity to bring home the bronze medal by one hundredth of a second. This shows how important each and every second is—and how every second can be put to use. How the timing can be improved. And who would know this better than a coach? This is what Dutee Chand's coach, a Dronacharya awardee, Shri Nagpuri Ramesh, is focusing on. And where else to find a coach but on the sporting field! In order to understand Dutee, it is important to know her coach.

V.S.: First of all, tell me about Dutee—what kind of a student is she?

Nagpuri Ramesh: What I want to say about Dutee is that she is a unique student, one who always likes a competition. She fights till her last breath. In my entire career I have only seen one such player who likes competitions with this intensity. Dutee is unique.

V.S.: So, what you are saying is that the tougher the competition, the better is her performance? Take us through your journey with Dutee, tell us what kind of training she undertook...

N.R.: I first saw her in 2009, when she was running for Under-14 and then it seemed to me that she had talent. Actually her sister Saraswati was a very talented player. One day, in the course of our conversation, I asked her, 'You have a sister who is very good—where is she?'

She answered that she had just left the hostel and was at home. Then, on an impulse, I said to her, 'Ask her to come here, and I will train her.' She responded, 'Sir, we are four sisters and our father is a weaver—all of us need to work in the family for our livelihood.' I had a friend, Parminder ji, who was also a coach. If a student comes from outside for training, three thousand rupees is needed for her maintenance. I spoke with my friend and he agreed to share this cost. We then brought Dutee Chand here and started giving her training. My initial thought was simple—make her into a national champion so that she can get a job and sustain her family in future. When she came to Patiala in 2012, within three months she broke the Youth Champion Records!

V.S.: Within three months only (surprised)?

N.R.: Yes, three months (chuckles)!

V.S.: Tell me, how strong is she mentally?

N.R.: As regards mental toughness, even as her coach, I have to learn from her rather than teach her (smiles). You would recall the hyperandrogenism problem that she had—that took her out of the Commonwealth Games. During that tough time she stood up for herself and fought against the whole world—and that is not easy at that age. She is also an inspiration for Indian girls. She is a girl who lives by the philosophy that when you are not at fault, there is no need to worry, and that you should fight.

V.S.: You have made an important point here. If you are not at fault, you love your game and are prepared to work hard on the techniques of the game, then there is no need to worry. The path appears by itself and so does the goal.

It takes Dutee Chand only a few seconds to cross her 100-m race finish line, but in order to achieve this, it took her years to train in preparation. Come, let us be a part of that training session today.

D.C.: One day it is endurance training and one day it is speed training, but no stamina training.

N.R.: More energy has to be spent on spins and energy training. The training is divided into phases. In the first phase, mostly it is Fartlek. There is long-distance running for 3–5 km. Dutee can run up to even 8 km. When it comes to weight training, the weight is lowered when there is a lot of repetition. When repetitions are done, there is an increase in weight. In the second phase we also do the plate run. Then there is the sand jump.

V.S.: We also spoke to the physio to understand how recovery is made after such intensive training regimen.

D.G. Arvind: Immediately after training is done, we start with stretching. We have facial release and strengthening programmes; we also have some massage sessions—they all help in recovery.

N.R.: Then around 12.30–12.40 she has lunch. A bit of relaxation follows. Then once again in the evening it is ground practice. Her best quality is frequency, which every sprinter should have. A sprinter is actually born with this trait. And, of course, as I have told earlier, she loves competitions.

Dutee explains to us why she is undergoing a particular training.

D.C.: Since I have kept the target of 11.1 seconds for 100 m, my current training is geared towards achieving that.

N.R.: The experience that I have with her is that when the whole world will say no, she will say yes. She is a born leader (smiles with a sense of pride).

V.S.: Tell me, Dutee ji, do you remember your childhood? I am told you used to run near the riverbed and spend time sitting there? Though you are still very young (smiles), still twenty, how often do you go back to your childhood days?

D.C.: Oh, very often (smiles). Sometimes when there is some problem in doing the correct training, I remember the way I used to run in my childhood. That strength has still not died in me. If you see, from my childhood I have laboured a lot. There was no ground near my village and I would always have to practise sprinting along the river. There was no sports equipment with me. I would have to get up early in the morning and practise running along the river. I would also run along the main road and I was scared because of the big trucks coming at great speed. I was scared and would often move to the side, but I still continued to run. Early morning when I used to run barefoot, the small pebbles and stones hurt a lot, but still I would run. Despite this, I have achieved all this and come so far. This, then, is the fruit of all my labour.

V.S.: An absolutely inspiring story! If you would have, at that time, run away from your fright and struggles, we would not be sitting here and taking your interview (smiles). Tell me, Dutee, how did you come by the idea of becoming a sportsperson?

D.C.: First of all, let me say that my elder sister Saraswati Chand is an athlete. Twice she has brought home medals for the country in the Olympic Police Meet. At that time she used to run in the village, while I was at home. She would come home and tell me, 'You come along with me and run too.' But at that time I did not even know the meaning of running. She only asked if annual sports were held in our school, and I said yes. She said, 'To get a good position in the school race, you will have to run; come, run with me.' So I started running. We had no cycle or car to reach school from home. The only choice was by foot, so I started running to my school (smiles)! This running to school helped me a lot. At that time, the prize that we used to get on coming first or second was slates and pencils and other things. Now we were too poor to afford such things, so the best way was to run, participate in events, win and get such prizes (big smile).

V.S.: Dutee Chand's elder sister was her inspiration. She had neither the bus, nor a scooter nor a cycle to take her to school. She did not even realize that being forced to run to school in a manner would one day be responsible for bringing her medals, awards at the national and international level and also breaking quite a few records.

You used to run barefoot. Do you remember the first time you entered the tracks with shoes on? And who gave you these shoes?

D.C.: I had asked my sister to get me a pair of shoes. When I ran barefoot, the pebbles and stones used to hurt a lot. So my sister gave me shoes. But then I did not know how to use them properly. So, initially, while running with shoes on, I had blisters all over my feet (chuckles). Then gradually it became a habit.

V.S.: Is there anything particularly special that you remember about your sister?

D.C.: Yes, my sister would always say this about me—perhaps the Almighty had sent me to this world for sports only, to break as many records as possible (shyly smiling). 'So work very hard and make sports your career and make the country proud. Work so hard that people like you and the country is proud of you.'

V.S.: You love travelling; this I know. But then tell me, do you like shopping? And what kind of stuff do you buy (smiles)?

D.C.: I love shopping for electronics goods—mostly stuff like TV and fridge, and automobiles—all expensive stuff (chuckles). I always fancied these things but in the beginning there was no money. But when I won a few competitions and money started coming in, I bought a few things. In the village our family was very often teased for being poor. So when I got some money, out of sheer anger I bought two cars (laughs). Not one but two (laughs again).

V.S.: Two cars! What are they?

D.C.: One is a Bolero and one is Enjoy—which gives me a lot of pleasure.

V.S.: That is a very interesting story and is somewhat similar to mine—because the first car I bought was a Honda City after playing for India. Incidentally, that was my first purchase for myself after earning. So I can say that both our choices are the same (smiles).

In the Commonwealth Games in 2014, you were not allowed to participate. What was the story behind it?

D.C.: At that time I was selected for three games—the Commonwealth Games, Asian Games and the Junior World Championship which was supposed to be held in the

United States (US) at that time. Just three days before the competition I was told, 'You are not eligible and cannot participate in the competition.' But nobody knew what was the reason behind my being asked to leave the competition. At that time I was very scared that I was being thrown out because of some doping problem. But after I returned home I got to know that I was asked to leave the games because of hyperandrogenism. I felt broken and very alone. People began gossiping, saying, 'Dutee is not a girl but a boy, and so she has been thrown out of the tournament.' I had left my family and worked hard to achieve laurels for myself and my country, and here I was, being treated like this by my own countrymen! I felt really sad.

V.S.: When did you decide that this is not to be tolerated anymore and you are going to fight against this?

D.C.: It was not possible to do it alone. I requested everyone, the state government and the Olympic Association, saying what they had done was wrong, and to give me some guidance and help me. But initially no help came from anywhere. Their standard reply was, 'What can we do? What is there in the rules will have to be followed.' It seemed the end of the road for me but then I met Dr Payoshni Mitra. She had followed my story and she gave me the assurance that she could help me. I asked her to come to my place. She came over and explained to me that she was a scientist and had done research on hyperandrogenism and that she could help me. She told me that if I could get help from the government, she would assist me in the case, since people had little or no knowledge about this condition.

We have not yet won the case, and it is still on. But

because of my fight, at least I got to play. The rules have now been changed to facilitate players who suffer from this condition, and because of this, three other players benefited. It felt very good that I had won what I had fought for.

V.S.: There have been a lot of ups and downs in your life. Who was it who motivated you and kept you strong?

D.C.: A number of people have helped me in my life. The most important is the financial support from KIIT University founder, Dr Achyuta Samanta. I got a lot of financial help from there. The state government and the Olympic Association also chipped in. For example, there is Gopichand Bhaiya (she is talking about the famous badminton player, P. Gopichand). When a case was made against me and I was thrown out of the hostel, he kept me in his own academy where I was free to train. He ensured that all my meals were free and he has not charged a paise even till today. So these are all the people who helped me and it is because of them that I am here today.

V.S.: Gopichand has a massive contribution in the life of Dutee Chand. So, from the bottom of our heart, we all extend our thanks to Gopichand ji who helped Dutee Chand greatly.

Tell me, Dutee ji, after this incident not only did you make a comeback, but also broke two records. How did you feel then?

D.C.: Nobody tries to make a record; the record just happens by itself (smiles). In order to get something, if one strives to do something bigger, then one can be sure that they will achieve something. See, I made 11.30 seconds my target for the national race which also happens to be the time to qualify for the Olympics. Now the national record was 11.38 seconds, which was then held by Rachita Mishra. So, naturally, when I am targeting for 11.30 seconds, I am bound to achieve something, and this was what happened. I finished at 11.31 seconds, which didn't help me qualify for the Olympics, but it did break the national record of 11.38 seconds (smiles). Then when I went to Walmart to compete, again the national record was broken and I qualified for the Olympics. In the heats also I qualified for the Olympics and established a national record (smiles again).

V.S.: (sighs) There are very few players who not only make a comeback, but also make a record alongside. Dutee Chand is one such person and we are proud of her.

What is the ultimate goal of your life, Dutee?

D.C.: I have two aims. One is to not only win medals in the Olympics but also to start an academy where kids can come and train, where they are taught how to win medals at that level. And my second objective is to become a leader and serve the poor of this country.

V.S.: The story of Dutee Chand is an inspiration for all of us. If there was someone else in her place, perhaps she would have broken down by now or accepted defeat. But Dutee Chand did not let herself become weak. That is the difference between a champion and a player. The dark clouds have moved away from Dutee Chand's life. Now she is ready to shine in every way. Now what's next is the next Olympics. Best wishes from our behalf to Dutee Chand. Jai Hind!

7

DATTU BHOKANAL

From a tiny drought-prone village in Maharashtra to rowing for the greatest sporting honour for his country, Dattu Bhokanal has come a long way. Overcoming crippling poverty and fear of water, Dattu finished where no other Indian rower ever had—13th overall in the men's sculls event at the Rio Olympics. This unlikely hero started out as a stone-crushing labourer to help out his father. After his father's death, Dattu joined the army to make ends meet, and was introduced to rowing. Today, he is training to bring home the coveted medal in 2020, and we will get a glimpse of how champions are made.

Come, friends, let me take you boating today. Surely all of you are wondering how long this frail-looking boat will manage to stay afloat in water. And where will the rower manage to sit? But let me tell you this, friends, this thin and apparently flimsy boat can move at a speed of 20 km/hr in the water. Today, I have come here to introduce you to someone who is an expert in rowing this boat. He is India's rowing champion, Dattu Bhokanal.

Virender Sehwag: Dattu, it is so strange that you come from a village in Maharashtra that is drought prone and dry most of the year. Coming from such a place, did you ever think that you would achieve so much and bring so much honour for the country?

Dattu Bhokanal: I had never thought that I would reach so far. Right next to my home there was a large pond which was dry for most part of the year. Naturally, a small path was created right through the middle of this pond. But during the months of June and July it used to be filled with water. Well, some of it. And I was so scared of water that when I used to cross this pond with my bike and enter this tiny stretch of water, my biggest worry would be, 'What if I drown (laughs)?' There was hardly any water, but this was the extent of my fear as far as water was concerned (smiles).

V.S.: (amazed) It is no less than a miracle that someone who was afraid of water became an expert in a water sport. How did this miracle come about?

D.B.: Things changed when I joined the army. Till then I was afraid of water. But I also have this childhood habit of fighting my fears. If I was scared of something, I would have to conquer and master that fear.

V.S.: What is rowing all about?

D.B.: It is a water sport—a race of about 2 km. If good time can be maintained, then one can become a good player; and believe me, it is an extremely difficult sport.

V.S.: Your family is into agriculture that involves tilling the land. From farming the field, whose idea was it to have you enrolled in the army?

D.B.: In 2011, when I passed Class X, it was my father's dream that I should join the Indian Army. Since I was tall and had a good physique, my father was sure that I would fit into the army very well. Unfortunately, in 2011, my father passed away, and then I thought to myself, 'I can at least do this much for him.' And then I joined the army to fulfil my father's last wish.

V.S.: How did you feel after joining the army?

D.B.: It was a different kind of pride—that I was able to fulfil my father's dream. But after coming here, gradually my mind started turning towards rowing.

V.S.: What is your rank in the army?

D.B.: At present I am a havildar.

V.S.: What was the inspiration behind your joining rowing?

D.B.: I have always believed in one principle—to do the best in whatever I am doing. This habit of mine stood me in good stead in the army and also when I was rowing. Just when my training was about to start, my coach, Subedar Quadrat Ali, had come there, and taking note of my height and physique, he asked me to start training for rowing. And then it all started. I followed whatever he said, maintained myself as per his directions. I would note down each and every mistake that I was making and would work towards rectifying it. Then he thought of formal training and that took place for 3–3½ months. Then there was a competition—inter-centre—and he asked me to participate in it. I performed well and won the gold medal. Then he focused more on me—on my diet, on my coaching. Then gradually I continued to perform well.

V.S.: And before joining the army, you had never rowed before?

D.B.: No, I had absolutely no idea about rowing—that it is a sport and an Olympic game (chuckles).

V.S.: A sportsman who had no idea about the game, no idea of the techniques involved, someone who became involved with the game only after joining the army, participated in the Olympics and came 13th. This is no less than a miracle. It is no mean task for any athlete to qualify for the Olympics. Added to it, to achieve the 13th rank is no mean task. Further, if all this is achieved only after about 3 years of training, it becomes very important to praise the coach as well as the trainer. Behind this rapid growth of Dattu is the dynamic coach Raghuveer Singh ji.

Raghuveer ji, where, when and how did you meet Dattu ji?

Raghuveer Singh: I met Dattu in 2012 when he had come for enrolment in the Indian Army. Even at that time I had noticed him, but I had not thought then that he would be training with us. Then, in 2015, when he had come down for rowing, his journey began (smiles).

V.S.: I had always believed that rowing was just a matter of using your hands properly.

R.S.: Sir, if you look at all the people whom I have trained, who have participated in the Asian Games and qualified for the Olympics, you will see one common feature. The rowers are not very muscular people. They do not build their muscles like bodybuilders do. And still, rowing is a sport of great strength. In rowing, all the strength from head to toe is used. When we sweat, we sweat from our toes too.

V.S.: How was Dattu as a student?

R.S.: Dattu was and is a very determined person. He has this determination to achieve something in the Olympics. It seems to me that in the next Olympics he will achieve something. The last time he reached the 13th position and this time in the finals I am sure that he will win some medal.

V.S.: I have heard that Dattu is very scared of water and swimming.

R.S.: Yes, sir (smiles)...I have a kind of link with Dattu. He comes from Nasik where there is very little water. I come from Rajasthan where the situation is the same. Initially, when I started rowing, I used to ask myself, 'What is this I am getting into? Am I going to drown or what?' I imagine it would have been the same for Dattu (smiles). I am an engineer and there is one thing that is of advantage to us. The moment we are inducted into the army, we are trained to learn swimming, to fight all fears related to water.

V.S.: In rowing, what are the kind of injuries a player faces and what measures are taken to rectify them?

R.S.: Shoulder, knee and back. These are the three vulnerable areas in rowing. Most of the injuries are because of back pulling and shoulder pulling, and some are knee injuries. The place of injury varies from rower to rower.

V.S.: When you first started your training in rowing, what were the memories associated with it?

D.B.: When I enrolled and was selected for rowing, on the first day, a 20-ft length of rope was strung from a tree. I was asked by the coach to climb up the tree by using the rope, but I was told not to use my feet, only my hands. I did that once and was asked by the coach to repeat the feat again. I again repeated the same drill. I did this five times, and when I completed my fifth round, my coach, who was by then amazed, asked me how I managed to do it five times. He said the regular practising players who train on a daily basis do it five times, and here I had, on my first day and without practice, achieved the same feat! I told my coach that I used to work in the wells in my village where part of my job was to climb them several times during the day (smiles). There too we only used our hands, hence, my hands were powerful.

V.S.: When was the moment you realized that you had become a proper rower?

D.B.: I qualified for the Olympics in Korea. It was the day after the qualification that we came to know that I had qualified. The information soon spread in the social media. Before qualifying for the Olympics when I used to row at different games and used to receive medals, nobody would come to know (chuckles). Since I was in the army, I could not speak to the press. After qualifying, gradually my coach sent out the message to the media and the word spread. Then eventually I came to know that I had become a rower and my coach said that henceforth I would have to work very hard.

V.S.: In the Army Rowing Node, what kind of facilities do you get?

D.B.: I have already practised in Hyderabad and Pune. I was given facilities everywhere—doctors, diet...whatever the problem, it used to be solved.

V.S.: Your boat is so narrow and thin and long—don't you ever feel scared rowing in it?

D.B.: (smiles) In the beginning I used to feel scared, but gradually that feeling has almost completely gone away.

V.S.: Now you know how to swim?

D.B.: Yes...

V.S.: So you are no longer afraid of water?

D.B.: No...no...not at all.

V.S.: Nowadays, there is a growing trend of marrying in a helicopter or in a plane—have you thought about marrying in a boat?

D.B.: My boat in which I participated in the competition is such that only one person can sit on it. It is impossible to marry in it, but I can definitely marry near a waterbody (laughs).

V.S.: Rowing is not a very popular sport in India. What kind of training is needed for it? How does a rower prepare himself?

To know all this, let us spend a day with Dattu while he is training.

D.B.: Rowing has become a part of my life and it is also very enjoyable. After getting ready around 5.30 or so, we come to the ground. Then we do ground training for some time—20–25 minutes of stretching, normal warm up and then for about 16 km there is a workout in the water, of about 12 km. Then it is normal stretching and workout. Then it's nap time till 2 p.m. Then we have our lunch and then again 4–6 is practice time.

R.S.: In the evening session we show the rowers some videos which focus on developing skills. If any player has any problem in his technique, or is facing some injury and wants to know why it has happened, we take the help of these instructional videos.

D.B.: The most important thing is that we do only such exercises which do not increase the heart rate. For the indoors we have hill training, box jump and leg pressing to develop our muscles. In rowing, while we have to do a full body workout, yet, the power in our hands and legs is not the same. We need more power in our legs, hence, the exercises are tuned to develop our legs and make them powerful. Then there is the bench press in which the power of the hands increases. Rowing is such a hard sport because where the pulse of others stops, the rowers' pulse starts from there.

R.S.: Seeing Dattu's willpower, I am sure that he will bring us something.

V.S.: Dattu ji, you have faced so many problems. Could you take us through your journey?

D.B.: Never have I been afraid of anything; like some players feel scared of competitions... if I was ever afraid, it was only for a couple of seconds. I know that if I put in all my effort, the result will be positive (smiles). And then there are divine assurances that constantly tell you to keep going.

V.S.: During your childhood, how did you spend time with your family?

D.B.: I did not spend too much time—and was always busy with my work. I was either in the fields or with my father.

V.S.: So even during childhood you would help your father in the fields?

D.B.: Yes, ever since I was in Class V, I used to help my father in the fields. No matter what the work, I used to help him, always.

V.S.: So did you not play any childhood games—like marbles, etc.?

D.B.: No, there was never any chance to play games. There was nobody to tell me—'Go on, son, play and have some fun.' I used to try and keep myself busy with all the work that was there in the house.

V.S.: Could you ever expect that a child who has never played a single game in his childhood would come 13th in a rowing competition in the Olympics? It seems impossible for me to believe. But the truth is that he joined the army and learned rowing; he then proceeded to make rowing his passion and brought honour to India in rowing in the Olympics. We hope that by working even harder, he will bring even greater accolades in the form of medals in the Olympics.

What changes did your father's death bring about in your life?

D.B.: At first it was an absolutely carefree life. Whenever there was any kind of work, people would directly approach my father—nobody came to me at all. There was no tension—only eating, working and relaxing. But after my father's death, everything changed. For the initial one or two months, there was a lot of tension—anybody who needed something now approached me directly. I was scared and wondered how to look at a given situation and how to face it. I was worried that I would not be able to accomplish anything. My mother was with me, and she would say, 'Don't worry, everything will be fine.' She would support me. Then I joined the army and gradually the problems that initially looked huge started looking easy and resolvable.

V.S.: Who all are there in your family now?

D.B.: I have two younger brothers. I have just married one off. My mother has also passed away. Now it is only two brothers and myself.

V.S.: What is the biggest dream you have for your family?

D.B.: When my parents were alive, it was a dream that they would travel in their own car. I had no car... I had absolutely nothing when my father expired. But now my only joy is that my brothers are happy because of me. Building a beautiful house for them—now that is my dream (smiles).

V.S.: The Olympics is the biggest dream for any sportsperson. Did you ever think that after four years you would be participating in the Olympics and would reach this far?

D.B.: I had never ever dreamt of this. It was an ordinary village that I came from—I had no name or fame. Nobody knew me and then all of a sudden everybody was cheering for me, asking me to go and get medals in the Olympics (smiles). It was a different kind of feeling.

V.S.: When you qualified for the Olympics, who was the person you first informed?

D.B.: Tears came to my eyes and I wanted to convey the news to my mother. But my mother had gone into a coma by then. She would open her eyes sometimes, but it was not possible to tell her anything.

V.S.: Your mother was unwell, in a coma and admitted to the ICU. But you still went for the Olympics. Would you tell us how you dealt with all this emotionally?

D.B.: I thought to myself, 'Go and achieve something worthwhile, so that your mother is happy. Who knows, she might even come out of her coma (smiling)!'

V.S.: Can you imagine...the mother of a sportsman is in the ICU and he qualifies for the Olympics. He cannot share this news with the person he wants to. He still goes to the Olympics, works very hard and comes 13th. Dattu had great mental strength and tenacity. I salute such sons of India.

So, Dattu, what did you learn in the last Olympics that you will be able to use in the following Olympics?

D.B.: No matter what problems arise, if you wholeheartedly pursue your goals and labour hard, you are bound to turn out a winner.

V.S.: When you went for the Olympics, did you feel that there was any shortcoming in you or something that was your big strength?

D.B.: The shortcoming was that I had not been able to practise enough. Practising for the Olympics is a different ball game altogether and the diet plan is also not usual. What was good for me was that I performed well in 3 months. If I had got at least 2 years, I would have been able to achieve the 5th or 6th position.

V.S.: So, do you find any difference in the Indian and international training patterns?

D.B.: There is a huge difference, and the difference is in the attitude. As far as Indian athletes are concerned, when a particular goal is achieved, they stop there. But this does not happen with foreign athletes. And I have seen this with my own eyes. When the final of the Olympics got over, it was 13 August, and I was just passing by the gym. My coach pointed towards the gym. And there these athletes who had just finished their finals were training hard! I looked at my coach in utter disbelief and he told me, 'You know what they are doing? They are preparing for the 2020 Olympics.' Can you imagine (in awe and smiling)?

V.S.: Do you feel any kind of pressure while representing your country?

D.B.: No, first of all there is great happiness that I am representing my country. I am going to achieve something good. I do not know about other players, whether they sleep at night or not, but I do. At the beginning of any race, I am a little tense, but once it starts, I come into my own. I will do whatever has to be done to win.

V.S.: After listening to Dattu's story, it is clear that it is not Dattu who needs rowing, but rowing that needs Dattu (smiles). He can spend his life in the army and carry on with his life, but will rowing ever get a player like this?

It is clear that a medal here or there cannot bring us an impressive medal tally. For that our government and sports authorities need to have an action plan and make sports like rowing popular like cricket or tennis—it is only then that the general public will take an interest in this sport and new talent will arise.

It is my hope that in the next Olympics, Dattu will bring us gold. We wish Dattu all the best. Jai Hind!

8

SHIVA KESHAVAN

Today, let us meet a player who is the face of New India. He is afraid of nothing. His speed is his constant companion and his hobby his thrill. This player represents the spirit of New India like no one else. He is a 5-time Olympian and the first Indian who represented his country in luge at the Winter Olympics. His name is Shiva Keshavan.

Virender Sehwag: Shiva, the game you play is a very interesting one, but very few people in India play it or even know about it. So, first of all, tell us something about it.

Shiva Keshavan: First if all, luge is an adventure sport. It can be played only in the hilly or mountainous regions. I am from Vashisht, Manali. Ever since childhood, we have been used to these activities and sports. Luge is basically a one- or two-person sledge, and we drive it at a speed of 150 km on the ice skating track which is of 1.5 km.

V.S.: 150 km/hr! It is like Shoaib Akhtar bowling.

S.K.: (laughs)...that too without an engine or brakes. The only option we have when we start this game is to reach the end and stop. We cannot stop midway.

V.S.: What is the difference between simply practising luge and practising it on actual luge tracks?

S.K.: The official name of this is artificial track luge. It is a 1½–2 km freezer and the ice is prepared very carefully so that all the athletes face the same conditions. But each track can be different depending upon the temperature or humidity—just like a cricket pitch. So, one has to understand many external factors to know the track one is going to compete on. A very important part is to go and practise on the track on which the game is actually going to take place.

V.S.: So, do you get an opportunity to practise there before the Olympic Games? I understand that just like in the Formula One races, there is first the practice on the actual track and then the race itself, isn't it?

S.K.: Yes, the format we have is very similar to that of Formula One. We have some practice runs. There are official training runs in which we have to qualify. Then their pole positions are decided on. The race takes place after that. Even for the Olympics there is a requirement that the athlete must take a minimum of at least 20 runs on the track before he can qualify.

V.S.: What is special about luge that attracted you so strongly and made you crazy about this sport?

S.K.: It is very strange that there are many people who regard luge as a high adrenalin and adventure game. But when I practise it, it is a very meditative game for me. The greater speed at which we move, it seems that time stands still. Time seems to stretch, and there is so much that we can do during that period. The human body is capable of doing so much. So, the way I think, this is the reason why I am so interested in this sport.

V.S.: So what you are saying is that when you are playing the sport at a speed of 150 km, you also mediate?

S.K.: It feels that the more the speed, the more are the things that move in slow motion (laughs). At least this is what I go through.

V.S.: (chuckles) Well, for me, a ball that is coming at 150 km/hr is coming at 150 km/hr (laughs). I can't say that for me it comes in slow motion (laughs again). But of course you are a master of this game. It seems strange, though, your philosophy.

S.K.: (laughs) No, no I have seen you—when the ball comes at that speed and you hit it so easily.

V.S.: To someone who is watching the game from outside, it seems that the player is hitting the ball easily. In fact Sachin Tendulkar has said the same thing that you did. When a ball comes at him at high speed he feels that he has more time to react. Everything freezes. It's strange!

We also heard while researching that you had a great deal of interest in athletics. So why did you join this winter sport and not something else?

S.K.: I studied at a boarding school, in Lawrence School, Sanawar, and a lot of emphasis was laid on sports. In school I was the captain of gymnastics and hockey, and athletics, long jump and hurdles—in the IPC I had also made records. So generally I used to take part in all-round sports. But when I got an opportunity to try this new sport, when the talent scout for the International Federation had come for the first time (and it was he who invited me to come and try this sport), I did. And I won the competition. Then he sponsored me to go to Austria for the first time and try the actual sport. That was where I savoured the speed and the adventure...And there was also danger—but I was greatly impressed by this sport.

V.S.: So, what was the thought process when you made up your mind to play the sports professionally?

S.K.: Once I was training in Germany for the International Federation Programme and there was a world-level competition at the time and I was invited to formally open the games. It was not to participate, but just to open. After all, it was the first time there was someone from India and they thought that it would add a bit of colour if a player from some country where this game is hardly known inaugurates the game. So I completed my first slope and just as I had finished and was preparing to leave, my coach came running to me and said, 'Do you know what you have done?'

I said, 'What? It was an ordinary run!'

He said, 'You qualified for this race!'

So what had happened was that since I was training with all these champions and learning, I actually managed to also compete with them. It was then that I realized that perhaps my career could start here in this field.

V.S.: So, while practising with them you managed to quality with them!

S.K.: It's like this—the qualifying time, our course is about 1–1½ km, is 7 per cent of the best time. Suppose the best time is 107 seconds, then it will have to be completed within 7 per cent of that time. So that was my first goal and I achieved it in that race.

V.S.: Do you remember how many seconds it took you?

S.K.: That race was for 51 and some seconds and I did it in 54 seconds.

V.S.: Do you remember when and where you qualified for the first Winter Olympics?

S.K.: The Olympic qualifying procedure that we have is that the top forty athletes are invited. It's not just that—after qualifying in the five qualifying rounds, the points start to accumulate. The first Olympics was a gamble for me because neither did I have the money nor the equipment to compete in so many races. I only had the ability to go up to five races. In each race I would have to compete and qualify; if I lost even one, then all my dreams of participating in the Olympics would be gone. But when we work so hard, even God takes our side. Everything went very smoothly and even in the first race, despite the fracture that I had, I qualified.

V.S.: When you represented India for the first time, what was it like? How did you feel?

S.K.: It was a very different feeling when I was carrying the Indian flag. For the first time I felt weight on my shoulders, the weight of the expectations of the people. I was now not an individual player but representing the entire country. I was just sixteen years of age at that time, just a child, and was the youngest player in the Olympics. But I thought, whatever the sacrifice, it was worth it.

V.S.: But in Nagano, when you participated in the Olympics for the first time, there was no coach with you. How was that experience? You were going to participate in the Olympics, but there was no coach with you.

S.K.: I have been representing India internationally for the past twenty-two years. And in all this time I have had a coach for the last three years only! Before getting a coach, I was practising on my own. My entire training has been the result of my own thoughts and planning—you can say, by trial and error, by taking note of what others did, by making friends with others and taking advice from them.

V.S.: So, who is your coach and where is he from?

S.K.: Duncan Kennedy is the name of my coach and more than a coach, he is my friend—because if he had been a professional coach I would not have been able to afford him (laughs). But after meeting me and listening to my story, he thought about how he could help me.

V.S.: After 2014, is there anything in which you think you have improved a lot?

S.K.: In 2014, for the first time I started focusing on scientific training, sports science and biomechanics. These are things I had never even thought about before. I would just practise for my games. But before that I did not have any guidance about how to practise. But ever since Duncan became my coach, it was as though a new door opened for me. I managed to see in what manner scientific training was carried out.

V.S.: Luge is not played anywhere in India. So when you are in India where do you carry out your practice?

S.K.: In order to practise in India, I have modified the sledge a bit. The blades that are beneath the sledge have been cut open and wheels have been put under them. So in this manner I can drive the sledge directly on the roads. The highway that is there between Rohtang and Manali, during the off season, when there is not much traffic, I practise there...

V.S.: You mean where the cars ply.

S.K.: Alongside the cars—and even overtaking them (smiles).

V.S.: What is the speed like?

S.K.: The speed comes up to at least 60–70 km.

V.S.: Isn't that dangerous?

S.K.: It can be dangerous if someone does not know the proper technique. There has to be proper planning and one has to wear a proper suit and helmet. I know the area very well, so I know what kind of a road it is, what curves I am likely to face and I can also anticipate from which direction cars are likely to come.

V.S.: So, can you slow your sledge, or should we say your small car, and also clamp down on the brakes? Are there any brakes?

S.K.: No (big laugh)! There is just one thing that is the heart of our sport and that is—there cannot be any brake. So, I thought to myself, 'Let me modify it in such a way that there should not be any brake when I am practising luge as well.'

V.S.: There is no suspension in this sledge of yours. What jerks or jolts take place, and how do you deal with them?

S.K.: All the vibrations that take place—they are the key factor for our sport. The more the vibrations and jolts, the less the speed. Our body needs to be so relaxed that the vibrations can be absorbed by it. So, thanks to regulations, there cannot be too many shock absorbers or things like that. Thus, we have to train our minds so that even though we are going so fast and there is so much excitement, our mind has to be calm and the body absolutely relaxed. The more relaxed the body is, the more are the chances of absorbing these little bumps on the road.

V.S.: Tell me something about your daily routine.

S.K.: Throughout the year my daily routine varies. The main goal of our sports is that we must peak at the time our games are actually taking place. Like when I travel in winter, I train for about 6 hours a day. Within that time, 4 hours is spent in technical training and 2 hours in physical training. In the summer, which we call a preparation phase, about 3–4 hours is physical training and there is an hour of mental training. Another phase of training, which is the first phase, is resistance. The body has to be prepared for whatever challenges come up—with long-distance running, stretching, flexibility, meditation and yoga. In sports, the mental aspect is most important. Also, concentration and learning how to do away with distractions. Not only that—also how to co-ordinate your breathing with your physical exercises. That is how we find our base. I think our training is in three phases.

V.S.: When you went to participate in the Olympics, all the finances that were needed by you had to be pooled in by yourself. How did you manage that?

S.K.: I tried many avenues for funds—asked for contributions from friends and family. Then when I started needing more facilities and equipment, I would go to various companies and ask them to support me—saying there would be branding and some advertisement and marketing. But it was not easy. In 2008, Abhinav Bindra won the first gold for India in the Olympics. It seems that from that point, the attitude of the country towards other sports has also changed.

V.S.: Whom do you regard as your staunchest supporter?

S.K.: In my sports career so far, I have had and continue to have a lot of supporters. However, my greatest supporter is my wife. She gave up her managerial job at a consulting firm. She left everything and became my manager. The first sponsor I got was because of her, because she knew the right approach to make, the kind of presentation that would appeal. We had sent applications to more than 100 companies and we got the first sponsor after that.

V.S.: Was your wife never afraid that the sports in which you were participating could result in serious injuries for you?

S.K.: She has a lot of faith in me. That faith also gives me a great deal of strength.

V.S.: I had heard that Italy had also wanted to confer a citizenship on you, but you refused. Is this true?

S.K.: This goes back to 2002. I used to participate in the junior circuit, but my aim was the senior circuit. Once the

Italian head coach approached me as he had come to know that my mother was Italian and I used to perform better than all the juniors that were with him. Then he asked me, 'Why don't you join the Italian team?' I did not even give too much thought to this because this was against the very reason I had joined a sport and wanted to play. I always wanted to represent India. A lot of people said, 'Why did you refuse? You would have got a good salary and good equipment.' All that is fine, but then I would not be at my own home now.

V.S.: Now that you have participated in the Olympics five times, the situation must have changed somewhat for you. So, has anyone come forward to support you?

S.K.: Yes, of course, now my supporters are Malcolm—who manufacture safety equipment for industrial workers, Hero Electronics, Hero Fin Corp and now I have just signed up with a new company—Deloitte. Now I believe there are many companies who understand the value of sports. We have so many companies and so few sports. So I believe that there should be no dearth of sponsors.

V.S.: How do you feel about having become an inspiration for youngsters?

S.K.: For me, now, when my competitive career gets over, my true career will begin. It is the knowledge that I have accumulated in these 20–25 years that will determine what I can impart to young players.

V.S.: A player can get the best results from his performance when those who support him nurture the same passion that he does. Shiva is lucky to have got the patronage of the safety gear company, Malcolm, that showed great confidence in Shiva and his sports. The executive director of Malcolm, Giriraj Mall, is now with me. We welcome you.

What kind of a player is Shiva?

Giriraj Mall ji: He is an extremely professional player and the youngest Indian Olympian who went forward, upholding the Indian flag—and in that cold. After Dhyan Chand, he is probably the second Indian player whose sports gear is in the Olympics Museum.

V.S.: As a sponsor, there are a lot of sports that you could have chosen to sponsor. You would have also got more publicity. But why did you choose Shiva?

G.M.: We manufacture safety items. When we talked to Shiva and observed that there are occupational hazards in his sport—he is following a vertical drop of 300 ft, the temperature is –40°C and he has to maintain a speed of 150 km with no break at all—we found he had many similarities with our company. We thought that there were a great many opportunities in unconventional sports for a sponsorship— and so we said, 'Let's get him on board.'

V.S.: What is the ultimate aim that you are seeking for Shiva?

G.M.: All that I want is that he does better than he has already done.

V.S.: Today I want to leave you with a thought. We, as viewers and as a country, only cheer for a sport that is popular. If the sport is popular, the government also spends money on it and we support it. But take the case of Shiva. He has participated in five Olympics so far and has also made records in many international competitions. But when have we sat in front of the TV and cheered for him? When has our government ever helped him? Still, it is not very late, and what has not happened so far can still happen. To awaken hope is the name of Umeed India. Jai Hind!

9

SANJEEV KUMAR

It is 'ability' that matters, not 'disability'. This saying truly defines Sanjeev. He serves as an inspiration to many like him, but his journey was not an easy one. Despite not having facilities like other international players, and initially training all by himself, he has managed to excel at an international level, becoming the only para badminton champion of India in the wheelchair 2 category. Affected by polio and belonging to a weak financial status, the only support he had was from his parents who somehow managed to arrange funds for his practice and tournaments. But his unbending dedication has always been his strongest asset. Let us discuss these hardships and struggles with the hope that Sanjeev will get the facilities and recognition he deserves.

Virender Sehwag: Badminton is supposedly an almost 2,000-year-old sport, which was played by name of battledore and shuttlecock in Greece, China and India. But in modern

India, badminton has started in Maharashtra, in the city of Pune. That is why this game was also known as Poona. Badminton is also regarded as the speediest racquet game because in a number of shots, the shuttlecock can move at a speed of more than 300 km/hr. This means that in order to hit the shuttlecock that hard, strength, agility and fitness are needed; and today the player whom I am about to introduce to you has all three qualities. He is strong, agile and fit. However, he plays from a wheelchair. He is the para badminton player, Sanjeev Kumar.

I am sitting in front of a player who has, without any kind of government support and without the help of any major sponsorship, won a gold in the Uganda Para Badminton International 2017 in the wheelchair 2 category. Sanjeev Kumar has achieved this all by himself, with his will and determination.

Sanjeev, first of all, tell me about your childhood that was spent in Punjab.

S.K.: My father was a volunteer in the education department. My parents tell me that when I was nine months old, I used to crawl and try to walk like kids of my age would do. Then I came down with a fever and you know how most of the doctors in the village are. I was given some injection to curb the fever, and after a few hours of its administration, my left foot grew smaller than my right. When my mother saw that, she became scared and spoke to my grandfather. He then took me to every doctor he knew. However, nothing could be done. Doctors told my parents and grandfather that I was inflicted with polio. Even then, my parents did not give up. They went for the operations, and two surgeries were done on me. We were waiting for my third surgery which could have treated my polio, but destiny had some other plans in store for me (smiles). The doctor who was to operate suffered a massive heart attack. Since the operation could not be completed, the foot became more and more asymmetrical, and also started to wither. To counter that, they had put iron clips on my foot, but boy, it hurt a lot. It was so painful to walk with those iron clips. I told my parents that it was getting very difficult for me to walk, since it was painful this way. I told them I would use a stick instead. Actually, my parents were concerned that I should not look like someone with a disability, and therefore, were eager for me to wear those contraptions to prevent my limping. But I went for the stick, and believe me, ever since this stick has come into my life, it has been magic. I have gained self-confidence and strength. Whatever I have achieved is because of this stick. When I have it, it seems to me that I am absolutely 'able'.

Sanjeev's mother, Kamlesh Rani, is proud of the fact that her son has become so independent so early in life.

Kamlesh Rani: Even as a child, Sanjeev had learnt to rely on himself and carry on alone. Even when he played marbles, he would insist on doing everything himself. His brothers say the same thing. We spoke to one of them, who said, 'He never appeared to be weak. No matter what game he played, he was always ready. He played cricket like a pro.'

K.R.: The most remarkable thing about my son is that he looks after the entire family.

V.S.: Tell me, how young were you when you began loving this game?

S.K.: When I was very young—it must be around Class VI in school. I always thought to myself that I wanted to become a cricketer. In the morning when school began, there would be young children playing about in the field. It was around '97—not a very long time ago. A ball came and struck me on the forehead. Then I went and asked my father if I could go home at half day (after all, he was a volunteer in the school). He asked if I was playing cricket on the grounds and I said 'No'. He said that henceforth I would also have to play. Gradually, I started playing so well that even a normal player would have difficulty in getting me out. And I was not using a bat; I was using my stick as a bat (big smile)! With every 6, my confidence was growing (big smile).

V.S.: Then why did you leave cricket and move on to badminton?

S.K.: It so happened that I became associated with a handicapped association of Punjab/Chandigarh. They asked me to play a match against Saket Hospital, Haryana. I thought—fine! Now, a match for the handicapped is a different thing altogether. I opened the innings and scored 88 runs off 37 balls!

V.S.: Buddy, even I have not scored that much.

S.K.: The boundary was small, sir ji! Then after that, I was told that there was the National Athletic Championships in Delhi. I said, 'Fine, let me try and play there too. Then I thought of playing the nationals too. I reached home, and from there, Delhi. I did not have a proper address—I had only been told that around the 24th or 25th, there would be a competition there. I was also told that at the Delhi station itself, a man would be waiting for me. And with just these directions, I boarded the plane to Delhi with no proper address and in the hope that a man would be waiting for me at the station!

V.S.: Did you find anybody?

S.K.: Yes, I reached and found the person. He mentioned the name of a school to us and we reached the school. There we met one Mr S.K. Dua ji. He made a call to the person who was in charge of the competition. I was told to participate in the event and I won the silver medal in the game of darts (smiles). In that same event one player told me that there was a game of badminton in the handicapped category and that I should try for that. I told myself, 'Okay, let me try badminton also (smiles). This happened on 25 January 2008. That was the day I decided that it was badminton that I would play. I was fascinated by the game. This was a game where failure and victory both would be mine alone. The strength would have to be found in myself and in nobody else.

V.S.: When your parents came to know that you were planning to take up badminton, what was their reaction? Did they not say, 'Try and play something else?'

S.K.: No, they did not say anything. Actually it was I who had decided in 2008 that it was badminton that I would be focusing on and nothing else. But I had never liked sitting on the wheelchair. Even when there was an operation on some day, I would get up the very next day and start walking with the help of my stick. The wheelchair was an impossible idea for me. I never liked it. But today the wheelchair is my career and it is my identity.

V.S.: We also spoke to his father, Virender Kumar, about his son's choice of career.

Mr Kumar: It was my dream that he would play and I would let him play. I just let him be. I never went with him anywhere. He alone has charted his journey. I applaud his courage.

Mrs Kumar: All people and children have a great deal of respect for him. Even the children playing cricket respect him and remark, 'Learn from him.' In the school where he used to study, teachers lecture the students that even with regard to studies, he never accepted defeat, and never gave in to the fact that he was handicapped.

V.S.: How many people are there who can make their weakness their strength? Nobody likes to be seated on a wheelchair. But did anyone think that one could sit on a wheelchair and play badminton? Will he earn accolades and bring medals? There is a spark in Sanjeev Kumar, that despite sitting on a wheelchair, he does not ever think of stopping.

Is it true that you stay very close to the border?

S.K.: Absolutely true! The border is about 10 km from our place.

V.S.: I see. You stay in a village that is so close to the border. How is life there?

S.K.: The village where I live is Telupura; this is in the district Fazilka. Life here is absolutely rustic and worry-free. Just eat, sleep and have a good time. Spend time with friends in the evening, play cricket and if you feel like, just go and visit the gurudwara. Simple life, filled with fun and frolic.

V.S.: It is a very comfortable life...

S.K.: Absolutely!

V.S.: What are the challenges you face while playing badminton? What were the challenges you faced while practising?

S.K.: When I started in 2008, I had already made up my mind that this was the sport in which I would have to make my name and fame. But the challenges for me were many. You see, the government does not pay so much attention to sports picked up by disabled people. So when I used to receive an invitation letter for a tournament, instead of getting excited about the whole thing, there was this tension that now I had to get the funds to participate in the event! It was a huge task. You need at least a lakh for practice and participating in any tournament. I used to get up early in the morning, wake up my brothers, prepare a list of possible donors and then go door-to-door to collect money. Some would give ten thousand, some fifteen and the rest I had to manage all by myself. I would say the situation is still more or less the same now. Sometimes I succeed in getting funds, and at times I have to miss the tournaments.

V.S.: When did you feel that you could play sports, specifically badminton, professionally?

S.K.: Actually, in the beginning, it was only the cement court where I could practise. In our school there was this cement court, but come to think of it, it is so difficult to move a patient's wheelchair even when someone is pushing it from behind (laughs), so imagine how difficult it was for me to move my wheelchair! The biggest turning point in my life was when, after practising on a patient's wheelchair, I qualified for the Asia Cup. There, one of my competitors in the pre-quarter-finals was an India champion. He had a very good wheelchair. I borrowed the wheelchair of a friend, and after beating him at the state level, I entered the quarter-finals. I lost in the quarter-finals, but I did not accept this as a failure because, after all, I had reached the quarter-finals. I thought to myself, 'If I can work even harder, it won't be long before medals will start coming in (smiles).'

V.S.: So, at a professional level, what kind of a wheelchair is used?

S.K.: A wheelchair plays the most important role when you are playing a game of this kind. The wheelchairs are very costly—up to 4½–5½ lakhs or so. The weight is 8–9 kg even without the tires. The wheelchair that I have is between 23–24 kg.

V.S.: So this means that an international player uses a 7–8 kg chair to play while you play using a 24–25 kg chair?

S.K.: The wheels for this are very hard to come by. The axle that I put in to lock the wheel is not in a very good condition and can come open any time because it is unlocked. Also, it is not available everywhere. It has become absolutely worn out and the tyres are on the verge of bursting. Now I have taken to changing the sides and playing. The biggest difference is that when I am playing sitting on such a heavy wheelchair, a lot of energy is wasted, while the player in front of me does not suffer from any such thing. My competitor's speed is usually good because he does not have to struggle with the heavy wheelchair. If I got such a wheelchair, I would certainly double my speed (smiles).

V.S.: This makes me wonder, in this huge country, is there no person who can fund a wheelchair for Sanjeev? I can say this for myself that I will certainly fund his wheelchair. At least we can give him one such chair that will help to bring home an Olympic gold in para badminton.

Sanjeev, tell us about your feelings when you represented India for the first time in para badminton.

S.K.: Oh! It felt so so good (teary-eyed). I started playing professionally in 2008 and in that year itself I qualified for the Asia Cup. It was a great feeling. From that day onwards my name has always been there as a qualifying player. I want to bring a medal for India in each and every category that I participate in (smiles).

V.S.: Either in singles or...

S.K.: Singles, doubles, mixed doubles...I have won 15 gold medals, 3 silver and 2 bronze. In international games, I have won silvers; in Uganda, I won a gold which India has never got in the wheelchair category.

V.S.: Sanjeev, tell me, what is the difference between normal badminton and para badminton?

S.K.: In normal badminton you have to play inside the entire court. For disabled athletes, there are some categories. For example, there is wheelchair 1 and a wheelchair 2 category. Since I have polio, I am in the wheelchair 2 category. Since my body balance is good, I am in category 2. Those who have a spinal injury are in category 1. Category 1 always competes with 1 and category 2 competes with 2. If doubles matches have to be played, then it is 1 and 2 combined. Or even 1–1 can play doubles. 2–2 cannot. Some matches are held in half court and others in full court. It depends on the disability, etc.

V.S.: If you play singles, then you play on half a court.

S.K.: The area behind the short service is out. You have to play in the area inside the box. If it was the whole court, then you would have the option of flicking and getting points from anywhere. Or else you have to continuously remain focused, and you also need stamina and speed because you have a very small margin for mistakes. Even if it lightly touches behind the short line, it is considered out and even on the sides it is out. For those on the wheelchair, it is very tough.

V.S.: What is a proper diet for you?

S.K.: Food and eating hardly makes a difference—playing is all that I love to do (smiles). When I go for a match, I do not have breakfast at all. All that I take is some juice—because if I eat too much, when I have to bend backwards for any shot, it puts too much pressure on the muscles. If I am hungry I can play and win; but if I eat, then all is gone!

V.S.: Where and when did you meet your coach?

S.K.: I searched on Google and found my coach. The first thing you have to do is find your mentor—because without a mentor you cannot learn anything. No competition can be won. Then I went to meet my coach—Surinder Mahajan. He was surprised to see me as he was not used to playing with a para player. I requested him to coach me and play with me so that I can get proper training. I told him that he should treat me as a normal player and if I didn't perform, he could ask me to leave. I also showed him the medals I had won. He was initially reluctant because he had never seen a player on a wheelchair. But then he decided to take me in, and from that day, I have been with him. I am what I am today because of my guru, my coach. Now my dream is to win an Olympic medal.

V.S.: Do you think there has been a qualitative change in your game after you have had a professional coach? Do you see any difference?

S.K.: The difference is of day and night, sir! I can now finish off a 21–point game sooner than before and with ease. And the interesting part is, my coach never accompanies me in any such tournament. I go alone (smiles).

V.S.: But do you sometimes feel that your coach should be there with you when you are participating in an event?

S.K.: Of course, I feel that need. For example, in 2013, I was playing an important quarter-final singles match in Germany. My competitor had a coach with him and I was alone. His coach noticed one weak point in me and my rival made good use of my weakness. If my coach had been with me, he would have pointed out my opponent's weakness too, and I would have made him run around in circles (smiles).

V.S.: It is no mean task to play without the guidance of a coach against a foreign player. A lot of strength and willpower is needed for this, and Sanjeev Kumar is not averse to hard work.

S.K.: Badminton is my life. If I do not play for even one day, I cannot sleep properly. Whatever labour I am putting in or the number of medals I am winning, it is all for my country. It is my dream that the flag of our country flies right at the zenith.

In the morning I get up around 6.15 a.m. After having a cup of tea, I pray to the Gods. Then after watching the news for some time it is time to leave. I change into my training clothes and go straight to the stadium. I reach there around 10–10.15 a.m. and training starts with warm up and fitting the chair. Then I have to practise manoeuvring the chair in the court. After that it is working to improve speed and accuracy. This is followed by playing some matches. The idea is to focus on developing movements in all directions, hitting and stroke techniques. We practise so much to ensure that no shot is missed. Accuracy with speed is the key.

Sanjeev Kumar's coach has very high hopes from him.

Surinder Mahajan: Sanjeev is a very good boy and very disciplined. The biggest factor for his wins is that he is very hard-working. The biggest strength of Sanjeev is his self-confidence. He has an overwhelming desire to do something. Our only wish is that he goes to the Olympics and brings us gold (smiles).

S.K.: During gym training, my main focus area is core strength conditioning, upper body and wrist and shoulder exercises. Maximum attention is paid to the wrists, and the shoulders have to be kept strong by virtue of strengthening the upper body.

V.S.: Now tell me, do you know what your strengths and weaknesses are?

S.K.: My strength is that I play an attacking game—my smash hitting, my dropping and tossing the shuttle and making the opponent move about in the court are some of the techniques. These are my strengths. I am not going to talk about my weakness in case anybody sees this interview and comes to know of it (laughs).

V.S.: What is your ultimate goal?

S.K.: My major focus area is the Olympics. I have to arrange a wheelchair for this. The time for the Olympics is drawing close and there is not much time. Olympics is like the Kumbh Mela of our country. It is a very important thing to not only participate in it, but win too. So, it is the dream of every player to play and win in the Olympics.

We spoke to India's foremost badminton champion, and he has an inspiring message for Sanjeev.

Pullela Gopichand (Chief National Coach): It is a very good thing that Paralympics is getting the place that it deserves, and in 2020, badminton will find a place in Paralympics. Sanjeev—all the best! You are an inspiration to a lot of badminton players, and wish you all the very best!

V.S.: Each and every facet of Sanjeev Kumar is an inspiration. He inspires because of his self-confidence, his ability to fight every situation and the never-say-die spirit. He is a true inspiration and an umeed for India.

On behalf of all of us, all the very best to Sanjeev. Jai Hind!

10

AYONIKA PAUL

Aggression is the most important factor for a player and his game because when there is a difference of only 1 second, 1 point or 1 run, then it is only aggression that is of use. But the game of the player I have come to meet today is exactly the opposite. For the air rifle event, there has to be a smooth coordination between the body and the mind. There has to be balance and stability and the whole body has to become one unit. Today, I have come to meet such a player who has fallen in love with the game. Friends, she is the future of our country, the future of this sport, the future of women's sports and the 10-m air rifle champion—Ayonika Paul.

Virender Sehwag: Ayonika, first of all, tell me, how and when did you come to know about shooting?

Ayonika Paul: At that time Rajyavardhan Singh Rathore had won the Athens Olympics silver medal. So that was when I heard about shooting. At that time I was pretty much a tomboy and I told my father that I had to hold guns and opt for shooting. Then Papa went to Ruia College and made some enquiries. He found the atmosphere quite good. Sanjay Chakraborty sir—who would win the Dronacharya Award later—was there at the time. I learned under him and did the basic course. It was quite good.

V.S.: You were also quite a champion in swimming.

A.P.: Yes, I was quite good at swimming and even now I do swim. I enjoyed swimming a lot. When I started shooting it was quite boring, initially. It was a 15–day course, but it took me 2–3 months, it was so boring. Then I participated in a competition and there something happened; I learned something about the trigger and I was hooked to the game. My score was not very high, but as I said, something about the trigger triggered my shooting career (smiles). The next morning I was at the shooting at 8 a.m. Those days I had to take the bus after school. That day I took a leave and went to the shooting range. I started at 8 a.m. and learnt something every day. Within one year, I was in the national team. That's how I got in and I don't know how I left other games.

V.S.: What is it about shooting that attracted you towards it? You were good at swimming and you also played basketball. Since you opted for shooting, there must have been something that attracted you to it.

A.P.: There is a kind of addiction with respect to shooting. You see, it works like this—if I press the trigger in a particular manner I will hit a score of 10. Then, in my next attempt, I missed that 10 score because maybe I was not holding the trigger properly. So I try again and hit 10! Like in childhood we used to try and hit rows of bottles with a ball—nothing happened at first, and then you gradually got used to it. That was how I got into shooting.

V.S.: What was the age when you got into shooting?

A.P.: I was about thirteen, in Class IX. During my boards, when I was just about fourteen, I was in the national team.

V.S.: What else did you do in your childhood?

A.P.: During my childhood, I was extremely overactive, and it was practically impossible for me to remain still in one place. I think I was quite notorious and would get into fights.

V.S.: You also beat up people?

A.P.: I beat up a number of boys, but now I talk of guns.

V.S.: Boys must be scared of you—the fact that you shoot.

A.P.: In school—yes.

V.S.: You have achieved so much at such a young age. How did you manage it all—your studies and everything else?

A.P.: I would like to talk about the dedication of my parents. I had some crazy ideas—I wanted to do this and do that, I wanted to be everywhere (laughs), and my parents always supported me. Whenever they wondered if I could do something, they always said that I should try. When I thought of going in for engineering because I loved maths and science a lot, I told my mother so. I was India no. 1 at that time. My mother said, 'You are doing well in shooting, but if you are to carry on both activities properly, you have to give them your full dedication. But I don't want you to let go of something because of something else; you leave your studies because of shooting or vice versa.' My mother worked out the timings for me—like in the morning from 4–7, I concentrate on studies. I rest for one hour and do my yoga and then I go for my classes. So my mother and father were always there to take care that everything remained in order. So there was a lot of dedication and time management from my parents' side.

V.S.: I did not know you were also an engineer!

A.P.: I am in the final year of my master's (smiles).

V.S.: It must be a little difficult to manage both, because I have seen that all the cricketers who have studied till Class 10 or 12 did not progress any further with their studies because they went deep into cricket. But you are no. 1 in shooting in India and have also participated in the Olympics; you are as good in engineering and are on the way to completing your master's. So, how do you manage to balance everything?

A.P.: If studies are done diligently, portion by portion, it does not become very difficult. It was most difficult for me during the World Cup because its timing clashed with my board exams. So I used to sit for my exams in the morning and after finishing the paper, would rush to the airport where my sister and father would be waiting for me with the luggage. I boarded the flight, played my game and came back on the day of the exams. It was crazy, but I loved it. I could not let go of either shooting or my studies.

V.S.: Behind the success of a player lies their hard work, and this is quite apparent in their performance. What cannot be seen is the inspiration and hard work of the parents. No player can become a good player without the motivation of the parents. So let us find out the mystery of Ayonika from her parents.

What was Ayonika like as a child?

Mr Paul: She was a very mischievous child and was really naughty (chuckles).

Mrs Paul: When she would get down from the school bus, it was quite clear to me that something or the other had happened in the bus. Something or the other definitely used to happen every day. Then, every day there was some quarrel in the bus or in school. Otherwise she was more or less quiet.

V.S.: When Ayonika first chose shooting among all sports, what was your reaction?

Mr Paul: The only factor that was important to me was that she should stay on the right track and do her duty. If she found success, it would be great. As long as she enjoyed herself, we let her go and play the matches.

V.S.: When did you realize her capability, her passion...that shooting is her passion?

Mr Paul: In 2008, when she was chosen in the India team for the first time, in the first World Junior Championship, she gave quite a good performance. It was then that I felt that there was something about her that would propel her forward.

V.S.: In order to fulfil the dreams of your daughter, what are the problems you had to face or battle?

Mr Paul: Shooting, by itself, is a very costly game. But when the child is showing good results, it is the duty of parents to support her in whatever way possible. We gave her as much support as possible.

V.S.: As parents, are you strict? That is to say about her shooting or studies?

Mrs Paul: When it comes to shooting, not at all, because she makes the plans herself. We don't know shooting.

V.S.: And are you strict about studies?

Mrs Paul: No, you see, she is very disciplined about studies. If 80 per cent has to be given, she gives 100 per cent—she gets up at 4 in the morning and studies for 2-3 hours. This is a habit instilled from childhood—study for 2, 3, 4 hours—but study properly and get up. Don't study the whole day. For shooting too, it is the same habit. In the morning session she practises shooting for 2-3 hours. She does not practise the entire day.

V.S.: How do you feel when you see your daughter playing for her country?

Mr Paul: What can I say—I feel so proud when amongst so many people I see my daughter playing for her country. In this particular event only two or three people represent the country. In my mind I feel like a really proud father.

V.S.: What dreams have you envisioned for your daughter?

Mr Paul: The dream is that the Indian flag should be flying high. Our daughter should achieve at least something that will allow people to remember her because of her achievement.

I believe that the way she is going about her game, she is there...she is there (smiles).

V.S.: Shooting is very technical. What are the techniques used here?

A.P.: It's a very precise sport in which not only physical but also mental aspects are taken into account. The slightest tremor in our muscles will take the 10th ring. There are 10 rings; the 9th ring is 0.5 mm. So, if there is the slightest change, it will come out of the target.

V.S.: While shooting, what are the minute factors you should keep in mind so that you do not miss your target?

A.P.: Shooting is a process for which preparations have to be made for a very long time. You have to be totally cut off from the world and everybody around you. For me it is also important to be a little hefty so that the balance remains stable. Because, on the match day, for two hours we have to remain standing in the same position. So, for that, during the time of training, we have to do at least 4 sessions of 2 hours each every day to achieve that stability.

V.S.: What is the weight of the rifle?

A.P.: 5 kg. 5.5 kg is the maximum for an air rifle. But 5 kg is the optimum.

V.S.: Standing with a 5-kg rifle in one position for 2 hours at a stretch and focusing on the target is no mean task.

A.P.: Yes, and the jacket and trousers also have a weight of about 10 kg and the shoes weigh 4 kg. So, remaining still with all that for 2 hours—and that too only during the qualifying period; during the finals you have to stand for one more hour.

V.S.: Ayonika is no less than a military personnel, who carries 5 kg of equipment, remains still for 2 hours and all the while remains focused on the target—that is truly difficult.

Tell me something, when you have taken aim and are about to shoot, in that moment, what is the right time or right procedure so that you can accurately hit the target?

A.P.: The trigger—first of all, the angle should be right—a little to the left or right and the entire angle of the gun changes. The grip should be optimum; the weight of the trigger is between 12–15 gm. Even if there is a little extra grip, there is a jump in the gun and the bullet goes and hits out. Along with that, it is also the angle of the elbow that has an effect on the angle of the gun. After you enter the centre of the target, you have a bare minimum microsecond. The full gun is moving, and for a microsecond it will stay there, and you just need to release the trigger. A microsecond can result in a 10.5 or a 10.0.

V.S.: That means at that time you might even have to hold your breath to hit the target.

A.P.: No (smiles), that's a technique that a player masters; how to breathe during shooting, because you can't stop breathing. It depends on player to player. For me it works best when I exhale.

V.S.: How important is breathing in the course of shooting?

A.P.: Breathing is the basis which keeps us in the zone of shooting. Pranayam after getting up in the morning is very important because it is from breathing that we get into the zone. We get into the full atmosphere of the shooting. When we are shooting, each and every breath counts. It is important that we are at the same place. We are there in the centre of the 10 and it is all because of breathing at the same time.

V.S.: When you are practising, do you have any idea what your heart rate is like, because if the heartbeat fluctuates, perhaps one might also miss the target.

A.P.: Of course it is very important—at the time of training we monitor it. But during a match it is not allowed. We just have an idea. During the finals, when the drums sound, there is an essential shot with which you come to know if it has hit the 10—whether you will be there in the finals or you will be creating a new record—the heartbeats increase to such an extent that you are able to hear your own heartbeat. You need to hear that, and between the beats, you release the shot.

V.S.: What is one essential element that has to be there in a shooter?

A.P.: Mental strength. Even the slightest self-doubt is a straight no for a shooter. When we are standing on the podium, and the national flag is fluttering high, that feeling cannot be put into words. We work so hard and put in so much labour—and that is only for the country.

V.S.: When did your international journey start, and how has it been so far?

A.P.: In 2007, it was my first Asian Championship. After that, most of the time I played all the World Cups because I was in the junior group and scoring like seniors. In some World Cups I was not permitted to participate because I had to go and play the Junior World Cup. The first time when I won the Junior World Cup medal, I realized that I could do it. I can fight at that level.

V.S.: Is there any special victory that you still remember today?

A.P.: The World Cup that took place in Maryborough in 2014—before that, the training was very good; but after that there was a World Cup in Munich, where I could not get into the finals because of a fraction of a second. There was an anger—that I could have made that fraction. That period was quite distinctive to me because I did not know what exactly to do in those 2 hours. In those 2 hours, if I cooled down, it would not be very nice, if I would be too hyper, that would also not be advisable. I asked my senior, 'What do you think?' She said that I had to just take one shot at a time and go on like that. The finals is not all that different. After eleven years of Indian participation in women's air rifle, I won the World Cup medal. So that match is pretty distinctive.

V.S.: Now tell us something about your coach—who he is, where he is and how you met him.

A.P.: When I began shooting, I was under Sanjoy Chakraborty sir, and in 2012, when I received support from the Olympic Gold Quest, I went and started training there under Thomas Farnik, who is a multiple-time world champion and a six-time Olympian. I started training with him and still do so.

V.S.: What do you gain by training under your coach?

A.P.: I get to know from him how it feels to be there at the highest level. It's the first-hand training, you can say, because he has just left shooting, and so I gained from his experience at the shooting range at the time of the Olympics. He would tell me about a particular tournament when the crowd was cheering his name and how he managed to remain calm, and concentrate. These are the lessons that are more important than what any sports science can teach you.

V.S.: The training for the 2020 Olympics must have started. What kind of practice or training are you doing?

A.P.: I am training for 36 hours a week, with 5 days of training—3 days of two sessions each and the other 2 days are made of one long session. There are 2 compulsory rest days where I need to recover and rejuvenate at the same time.

V.S.: What is your ultimate goal?

A.P.: The 2020 Olympics.

V.S.: Thanks to Umeed India, I get the opportunity to meet a lot of champions and players. But today, after meeting Ayonika, my attitude and thoughts towards the other sports have become very positive. The manner in which our younger generation is looking away from conventional sports and drawing closer to other sports, it seems to me that the medal tally of India is likely to spiral upwards. I wish Ayonika all the very best for the future. Let her achieve the highest pinnacle of success in life and also win many medals. Jai Hind!

11

ANNU RANI

Javelin has been practised by the human race since the Stone Age. In order to appease his hunger, initially, man used to hunt with a spear or a javelin. Later on, during wars, it became the main weapon. Greeks introduced it into the Olympics and it became a part of the Olympic Games. Now it has fast developed into a dynamic game. I want to give the credit of making javelin popular in India to the champion of the game, Annu Rani. Today, I have renamed her and will call her Javelin Rani from now on.

Virender Sehwag: Annu Rani, agreed?

Annu Rani: (delighted) It is a matter of great pride for me that such a renowned player and star like you has given me a name—that's a great honour for me.

V.S.: Thank you for teaching me javelin, Annu.

A.R.: Thank you.

V.S.: Annu, first of all, tell us what is a javelin, and how it is played.

A.R.: Sir, a javelin is a long baton of bamboo. Initially, if we begin practising with a bamboo it is good, because there are fewer chances of injury. Generally, a javelin is 600 gm in weight. As our level of competence increases, the material of the javelin changes from aluminium to carbon, etc.

V.S.: So you have to throw a baton of 600 gm—and this is a javelin? Sounds simple. How much strength is needed to throw the javelin?

A.R.: Sir, javelin is a sport in which there are chances of grave injuries of the elbow, shoulder, knee and ankle. In order to throw, our entire body is used, and so there are chances of developing injuries. It appears to be easy, but it is not. In the beginning when I picked it up I thought it was very easy and I could throw it to a great distance. I remember picking it up and throwing it. I fell down, much to the amusement and merriment of players around me. I was so embarrassed, but also realized that I should not treat this game as simple.

V.S.: How does one throw the javelin?

A.R.: There is a run-up of 30 m. You have to run that far and then in the last bit apply as much effort and force as possible.

V.S.: Has it ever happened that you have aimed the javelin in one direction and it has actually gone elsewhere?

A.R.: Yes sir, it has happened. There is a grip, and when that becomes loose, the angle changes and it can fall this way or that. When I first started, a coach used to train me there—by mistake, the javelin got embedded in his foot!

V.S.: The coach was injured?

A.R.: I asked the coach to move back a little, but he asked me not to worry as there was no chance that the javelin would go so far, and so he did not move. But when I threw it, it hit him (laughs).

V.S.: He did not try to catch or avoid it... You threw with such force that it hit him?!

A.R.: Yes, he still remembers me (chuckles)!

V.S.: Annu, tell me something about your life—what you were like as a child, how you learnt javelin, what problems you faced—tell us something about all that.

A.R.: Sir, you know how the lives of girls in our villages are. They grow up, learn housework and then get married. But I didn't want this life for myself. I wanted to get out of that environment. So one day I asked my father if I could join some kind of sport. He was very angry and asked me how I could think of playing, since I was a girl. He was against me joining any sport. But I am one stubborn person. Also I am the youngest in my house and can throw tantrums. I kept on crying and stopped eating for days, till they let me join some sport. Ultimately, my father relented. He had thought that maybe I was not serious about sports and it was just a passing fancy and that I would return to living a normal life (chuckles). Papa had not realized that I was planning to go far.

V.S.: That you would be the first woman in this sport to participate in the World Championship or become a world record holder (smiles). So then what was the reaction of your parents when you made a national record?

A.R.: Initially, my father did not like it, but after that he supported me a great deal. My father and brother both supported me a lot. There was a time when I was halfway through my training. My father said that they could not ask me to discontinue sports since I had gone too far. At that time my father borrowed money from his friends to sustain me in this sport financially. It was a huge struggle.

V.S.: So, who told you about javelin?

A.R.: Javelin, sir, was a sport in our school, and there were three events. If I brought home gold in all three, I would win the championship and get a scholarship as well. So my PT sir told me that I should participate. So that is how I started. I also said to myself, 'Javelin is light, and anyway, I can run and throw it.'

V.S.: Where did you get the bamboo from? Did you make it yourself or did the school authorities give it to you?

A.R.: At first, the school authorities did so. But then I practised to such a degree that I broke a number of javelins. The teachers said, 'She breaks so many, we will not give her any more.'

V.S.: When you took up javelin as a profession, what were the problems that you had to face?

A.R.: To begin with, I did not even have shoes to wear. A kit was needed, and even that I did not have. The shoes with spikes that are needed for throwing the javelin cost around

10,000–11,000, and that was also not there. So, initially, there were a lot of problems. I told my father about the spike and he replied that my demands were growing—where would he get the spikes from (chuckles)? He was okay with buying me regular shoes, but shoes with spikes were way out of his budget. But then he managed somehow.

And then, one day, I went to my school. I had this Nike bag which had my shoes with spikes and mobile and other things, and it got stolen! I was so scared as to how I would face my father. That I had lost everything like this. I tried to avoid going home, but I had to. And naturally, I got a good scolding from my father.

V.S.: I can understand Annu Rani's problem in buying shoes worth 10,000 INR because when I was a kid and got my first shoes, it was around 400–450 INR at that time. I did not have the money for even that. The player who has to struggle to buy shoes or equipment learns the worth of her/his sport. Annu knows just how hard she has to work to move ahead. I also had to work hard in this manner, but Annu Rani's struggle is definitely more than my struggle.

Is there any player or personality who has left a deep impression on you, so much so that you try and behave like that person, emulate him/her?

A.R.: In my life, the major contribution is that of my coach. When I was a kid, I came to know that there was a boy named Kashi and he was participating in the Commonwealth Games. Some media person asked me who I thought would win a medal for India in the Commonwealth Games, and I said Kashi sir. He had struggled a lot and put in a lot of hard work. Sir is my inspiration. He later started coaching me.

V.S.: So your coach is your inspiration and you are very happy to be undergoing coaching under him?

A.R.: Yes, I am very happy.

V.S.: Does he ever scold you?

A.R.: Oh yes, I even get smacks!

V.S.: Your coach Kashinath...where and when did you meet him?

A.R.: In 2012, in the Commonwealth Games, he, too, created a history of sorts. He won a bronze medal and had come to Meerut. Father would not let us girls go anywhere, saying, 'What will you do by going there?' and all that. My brother went to Meerut. He talked to him and requested him to coach his sister. And that is how he began training me. He suffered a shoulder injury and he had to leave sports altogether but then he started training me full-time. A contract was then signed with him and I came here.

V.S.: After you met your coach Kashinath and he decided to take you up, how much difference did it make to your performance?

A.R.: When I first came here, I was able to throw till 45 m. But after training with sir, I could throw till 62 m. So, that is quite an improvement.

V.S.: As of today, what is your best performance?

A.R.: So far in competitions my best is 62 m, and in the ground I have achieved till 64 m.

V.S.: That means during practice you have thrown till 64 m?

Tell us something about the bonding that is there between your coach Kashinath and yourself.

A.R.: Sir is like my father and cares a lot about me. If there is something that I want to eat from outside, he will get it for me and ensure that it reaches me in the hostel. He really does care a lot.

V.S.: So you would say that there is very good bonding. It is the relationship between a father and his child.

A.R.: In my life he is a very important person. Sir used to participate in sports, but he could not go forward because of his injury. So all my effort is to fulfil the dream that was not possible for him.

V.S.: Friends, as soon as the name of a coach is mentioned, the image of a senior player comes to mind. But Annu's coach is very young. His contribution, guidance and support is no less than that of any senior coach. He has been the national champion 14 times and is the only Indian player who has brought home the bronze medal from the Commonwealth Games—Mr Kashinath Nayak.

What was special about Annu that you decided to become her coach?

Kashinath Nayak: When Annu came here in 2013, she did not know anything—picking up weights or even the ABCD of javelin. She only knew how to throw the javelin. I had observed even when I was a player that she had talent but could not find a proper coach or guidance. A lot of people told me that this girl was short and she would not be able to do much. 'Why are you wasting your time on her?' My response had been this—height is nothing. Sachin Tendulkar is short, but people consider him God! Annu works very hard and with a great deal of sincerity... Let's see how far she can go. She does whatever I ask her to do.

V.S.: How is Annu as a student?

K.N.: She has been with me since 2013 and has never missed a training. Even if she didn't keep well, she would not tell me and still turn up for training. I remember one incident when she was not well but she still continued with her training. She was doing some exercise and she was dizzy and fell down and hurt the back of her skull.

V.S.: Annu does not let any illness or injury let her miss her practice. She does not tell anybody about it and is very dedicated towards her sports.

K.N.: Yes, yes. She would never tell anyone if she suffered from something, lest it affected her training. Now, however, I know her so well that I understand with each and every movement of hers what is going on within her (smiles).

V.S.: During training, is there anything special that happened with Annu that you still remember?

K.N.: One day, her father had come, and she was practising throwing. Her father said, 'What is this? Ever since I have been watching you have been throwing only 60 m.' Again she threw, and it went till 60 m. So I told Annu that now was the time to show her father what she was capable of. By that time she had thrown some 30–40 times and had thrown at a distance of 57–58 m. She told her father to move back till 65 m and just like that, she threw the javelin at 64 m! I felt if each day was like this for her, anything was possible.

V.S.: When you were a player, you won so many medals; when you coach someone, and they win medals, how do you feel?

K.N.: When I was a player my heartbeat did not increase so much; but when I see my students play and throw, my heartbeat probably goes up to 200! Last time when she qualified for the World Championship here, in her very first throw, she hit 61.86 m. I cannot express the joy I felt. I embraced everybody I met, and it was a joy beyond all boundaries. I almost started weeping with joy—this is what happens when any of your students do well.

V.S.: You and Annu passed through a phase in 2015... Tell us about that.

K.N.: In 2014, when she won the bronze medal in the Asian Games, she got the sponsorship and the government began to focus on her. All of a sudden there were sponsors and too much attention on her. The result of this was that she got scared of injuries and hence stopped taking any risks or making that extra effort lest it should make her prone to injury. I was also under pressure since she was the only player I had at that time who was throwing at more than 60 m, and if she was injured, I would be asked a thousand questions. So both of us became cautious, and as result, our performance in 2015, after the Asian games, dipped.

V.S.: What is Annu's training schedule like?

K.N.: There is a daily training of 7–8 hours. And then there is training with equipment. I have seen cricketers like Sachin sir train. I have seen him swinging two bats inside the pavilion. So I applied the same technique with Annu. I ask her to start throwing 800 gm first, which is for boys, and then after some time 600 gm, which is meant for girls, and it became easy for her. Last year, in seven steps, 56 m was her best, and this year she did 63 m. This means she improved by 7m just because of doing this.

V.S.: What is your ultimate goal for Annu?

K.N.: I keep reminding her that she is also like the girls shown in *Dangal* (smiles); that she too has come from a village and she too can do it. Just bring back the Olympic medal for the country—the rest is all up to the Almighty, whether he thinks she is worthy or not. Once you get the medal, you will get everything.

V.S.: So, the ultimate goal for her is the Olympics.

K.N.: It is only to win that—there is no other task. For Annu Rani, the practice begins at 6 a.m. It continues till 10 o'clock.

A.R.: In the morning, first of all, we run 2 rounds; then follow it up with several other exercises. Then the workouts begin. In the workout sessions, we focus on building strength. There are a lot of exercises to improve strength—the squat, the snatch and the pullover. All this is practised.

K.N.: Then there is stretching and massaging. Then vitamins and proteins are also taken so that the body has a better chance of recovery. After taking proper rest, the second round of training begins from 4 p.m.

A.R.: In throwing, we focus on the technique. If the

technique is proper, then the range and distance are exact.

K.N.: Then the score is 60–70. Then, after that, there is weight training.

A.R.: There is some amount of help from weight training—just like with the distance we throw the javelin. If the shoulder does not have that power, there are greater chances of injury. So, in weight training we develop our power; our muscles are developed.

K.N.: Annu is extremely sincere, but the little flaw she has is that she tends to forget. What is in her, what she can do, she sometimes is not able to do. During practice she makes 64–65 m. If she is able to do that in the competition, there is no doubt at all that she will win in the Olympics.

V.S.: Annu, how did you feel when you played for India for the first time?

A.R.: Playing for one's country is a dream for any sportsperson, and there can be no greater moment than when you bring back a medal and hold the flag of the country proudly.

V.S.: When you play for your country, do you feel any kind of pressure or stress?

A.R.: The expectations of the entire country accumulate, and that does create a little tension.

V.S.: There are also the expectations of the folks at home—and that too creates a little bit of pressure.

A.R.: My father also does not like it if I do not break any record. He says, 'Just bring home the Olympic medal, that's all.' His expectations have also grown (chuckles).

V.S.: (laughs) So, along with you, his aim has also grown?! As soon as you broke the national record, the demands of bringing home the medal in the Commonwealth and Asian Games began. You have broken and made so many national records—what else remains for you to achieve?

A.R.: Unfortunately, sir, India has a history of never winning a medal in athletics. So that is my target—that I create this record and bring home a medal for India.

V.S.: Be the first woman to bring home a medal in athletics? I hope that you will be able to do this—because you are stubborn. If you have made up your mind, then you will definitely achieve something.

Annu is a girl hailing from a small village. She began without any formal training in javelin. She is the Annu who got up again after sustaining injuries. If she is not the one to win an Olympic medal, who will? If she is not the one to make a world record, who will? This is my expectation from her...this is India's expectation. Jai Hind!

12

B. SAI PRANEETH

This is a badminton court and Virender Sehwag is swinging his racquet. Opposite him is Sai Praneeth, India's top badminton payer. After a few volleys here and there, an impossible thing happens—Sehwag scores a point against Sai!

Virender Sehwag: I also know how to turn a racquet, Sai, and not just the cricket bat (chuckes).

Sai Praneeth: Absolutely, sir (smiles)!

V.S.: Thank you for giving me a couple of points (smiles back).

Friends, it is not possible that on a sports page there is no mention of badminton. In international competitions, it is almost impossible that Indian players are not in the top three echelons, whether it be Saina Nehwal, P.V. Sindhu or Parupalli Kashyap, or today's special guest, Sai Praneeth. Welcome to Umeed India, Sai.

I have noticed that all the shuttlers or badminton players come from Hyderabad. Tell me, what is so special about Hyderabad?

S.P.: In Hyderabad, there are champions and good coaches, and so the juniors aspiring to play the game also have an advantage, since they get this kind of exposure...and it carries on like this (smiles).

V.S.: How did you start playing badminton?

S.P.: Actually my aunt used to play badminton. She was a national player. She used to play with Gopi sir and all. So, because of her, my grandfather introduced me to badminton. There was another stadium, LB Stadium, where Gopi sir and others used to play. My grandfather used to take me there and show me how the game was played; he used to tell me about Gopi sir and how great a champion he was...

V.S.: When did you first start playing badminton professionally?

S.P.: I first joined summer camp and then gradually became a regular player. In Class X I got my first All India rank, and I was a national champion in the under–13 and under–16 categories. Then I thought I had to do this, and since then badminton has become my career.

V.S.: How did you feel when you first represented India?

S.P.: 2011 was the first time I represented India in the under-19 category. Before that, Kashyap and Saina would wear India T-shirts and I would look at them and think, 'When will I wear this India T-shirt (smiles)?' I will never forget the day I first played for India—it felt really good.

V.S.: How was the experience for you—training at the same academy where Saina Nehwal, P.V. Sandhu and Kashyap trained? How was it practising with them? What was the experience like, and how motivated were you?

S.P.: I was so lucky to have trained with champions like Saina, Kashyap and Sindhu. I was highly motivated when I saw them play—there was also an impetus for us to win. In the men's category, Kashyap is the seniormost. I talk to him a lot and he has a varied experience. He explains to me how to handle the shuttlecock. We also discuss a lot of things amongst ourselves. If there are certain difficult situations, how to react to them... Since someone as experienced as Kashyap is with us, in that context, playing in the academy and seeing all these things works in our favour...it is definitely advantageous.

V.S.: How did it feel when Gopichand started coaching you, and what was the experience like during the process?

S.P.: Gopichand sir started coaching in 2005. So, I was in one of the first batches of Gopi sir. Gopi sir is so dedicated, and it is because of him that we are where we are now. Indian badminton is extremely popular now. It feels so great being under him.

V.S.: How is Gopi sir on the court? Is he soft or strict?

S.P.: While training us, Gopi sir is serious, very serious. But outside the court it's all fun. In the court too, it is somewhat relaxed. But as soon as the game begins, his attitude will change (for the better). By nature, he is a disciplinarian.

V.S.: Have you ever got a scolding?

S.P.: Many times! Since the time I was young, many times. I am a bit slow on the court and to stop me from being slow, he shouts at me. If I am slow he shouts so loud that I become alert. This has happened many times!

V.S.: Coaches have to be strict because they know the right manner in which to handle their students. If your coach is not strict then perhaps the desired results will not be achieved. That is why they are strict. My coach was also very strict and so was Tendulkar's, and here, Gopichand is also very strict.

Since your training in the academy, how much improvement has there been in your badminton skills, and how much has changed?

S.P.: The game is changing fast, and the techniques are also changing. Whenever the coach comes with us for international tournaments, he keeps looking all around. Whenever he sees something new, he immediately comes to us and tries to implement it in us. As he is an international player, he is very observant and can catch on very fast what is happening in world badminton. There are many advantages like this. Sir knows all the top players of the world and how to beat them. He keeps on drilling this into us many times. So we feel great that we are all training together under Gopi sir.

V.S.: A player works very hard and labours for his particular sport. But one coach labours for all his students. Saina, Sindhu and Sai Praneeth, they are all known to you now. But it was their coach Pullela Gopichand who was the first to recognize their talent. We are privileged to have Gopichand with us now.

We all are aware that you were the coach for Saina Nehwal, Sindhu and Srikanth. But who was Gopichand's coach?

Pullela Gopichand: Actually, I have had a number of coaches. In the beginning I had Hamid Hussein sir. I had gone to the stadium for cricket. I did not get admission and so I joined badminton. I said, 'Sir, I want to play.' And he asked, 'Are you sure? There are few who come to play badminton.' Then there was Aryu sir who was my coach. He was the one who actually taught me about sports and fitness. Then there was a Chinese coach who had been brought by the Government of India during '91–'93. I attended a lot of camps under him. There were a great number of coaches, and it is clear to me that each one made a lot of contribution to my training.

V.S.: How did you feel when Saina Nehwal and P.V. Sindhu won medals in the Olympics? Please share your feelings with us.

P.G.: An Olympic medal is something very dear to every athlete. In 2003, I had gone to Sydney and played there. It was a dream that I would return with a medal, but it did not happen.

The relationship that I have with an Olympic medal, the closest that I can get to it, is if one of my students wins. It's a great feeling.

V.S.: There is a question which perhaps I, your fans and everybody wants to ask—between points, when you talk to your players, what do you say to them?

P.G.: There is very little time to say anything, but there are a couple of things—to point out the good moves the player has made, because sometimes they play well unknowingly—so you tell him what he is doing well. Also, perhaps, the two things he should avoid doing. Then the call comes—time up, they have to leave. So I think there is very little we can say. Most of the time it's just building confidence—motivation. Sometimes it is dispelling fears—if you lose, it will not make any difference, but be brave and fight it out. So, it depends on which player you are talking to and the timing of your talk.

V.S.: When and where did you meet Sai Praneeth for the first time?

P.G.: In April 2004, along with a group of 25 people in Kachhiwali Stadium, we started the academy. In this informal manner, on the auspicious occasion, we said our prayers and announced that we would start training from the next morning. Sai Praneeth was there in that first batch. I always felt that he was talented.

V.S.: How is Praneeth as a student?

P.G.: A little laid-back, but the last few months have been a revelation. Since the time he realized that with hard work, results can be better, his attitude, body language and whatever else goes on in his mind has changed—because all of it has an effect on this sport. The way he has been managing everything has been fantastic. That is something I really like about him.

V.S.: Is there anything special about Praneeth that distinguishes him from the other students?

P.G.: On court, his intelligence is the best is what I would say. In the World Championship, there are two rounds and in both the rounds you could see his urge to win. His spirit of not giving up is something fantastic.

V.S.: Is there any weakness of Praneeth that both of you are working on to improve?

P.G.: There are two areas which definitely need improvement—movement and fitness. In both these fields there can be a definite improvement. So far as strokes and on-court intelligence is concerned, I think he is somebody who has it.

V.S.: For the coming tournaments, what kind of training are you preparing Praneeth for? What factors are you working on?

P.G.: In the last couple of months, the manner in which training has been carried out, the Indonesian coach who was with us—Emilio—his support and everything else has been fantastic. Whatever is working out, I think we will continue with the same things with greater intensity; and we are hoping that in the coming tournaments we will have even better results.

V.S.: If I ask you that in the coming 2020 Olympics, where do you see Praneeth, what hopes do you nurture for him, does he have the capability, and will he be able to bring home the medal, what would you say?

P.G.: Definitely! He is somebody who is immensely talented, and he has the potential to get us the medal.

V.S.: How has your journey in the world of badminton been so far, Praneeth?

S.P.: There have been ups and downs—sports is like that. Till under-19, I was no. 1—so there was nothing to think about. Then, initially, when I came into the senior group, I found there was a great deal of difference between juniors and seniors. Then I found it very difficult to bridge the difference.

V.S.: As Sai has said, there is a great deal of difference in moving up from the junior to the senior level. I, too, found the same after I played for India in the Under-19 World Cup. That gap is a very big one and it is only the player who is truly talented that will survive. There are many players who come up from the Under-19 team and after that are not able to do anything much. For that, a lot of hard work has to be done—like Sai is doing. After becoming the Under-19 India champion and no. 1, he came to the senior level and quickly filled the gap.

In the Super Series, you defeated Lee Chang Woo and made your comeback. After that, even in the Canada Grand Prix, you played well. Tell me something about your experience in the Super Series.

S.P.: Lee Chang was actually world no. 1 and no one was able to beat him. I was the first, from India, to do so. It felt very good. But playing in the next round with some other player, I lost a close match and felt very bad because it was a major tournament—the All-England Championship. Then, after working a little harder, I won the Canada Open. I had really worked hard for this tournament, training for 1–1½ months...

V.S.: Sai, tell me, what is more important in the game—brain reflex or muscle reflex?

S.P.: Both are important because when we enter a game, there are different types of opponents—like as an on-the-spot reaction, whatever tactics he is using, we too must know about it. We must also keep track of the stages of the matches because when the game is about to end, there is an energy drop. The energy will come from the muscles, so it is important.

V.S.: Tell me, what techniques are used in order to improve the smash that you'll use?

S.P.: There is weight training, and during practice, for 15–20 minutes, there has to be a continuous volley of smashes. For power, one has to go to the gym. For the muscles that are required to be built, with the correct workout and with general practise, there is improvement.

V.S.: If I compare cricket to the smash shots, say when we hit a cover drive, straight drive or any other shot, we take more than 10–15 minutes practice to hit that shot in the match. In the nets we practise at least for 100–200 balls for that one shot. Do you do the same with the shuttle?

S.P.: Yes. So we have a number of shuttles in our hands and we keep hitting them...keep smashing them...we aim for that perfection and power...

V.S.: How much balance should there be between attack and defence when you are playing a game?

S.P.: Both are equally important! It is important to have balance because to win a point I will have to attack and if I lose the shuttle, then defence will be needed. Both are important.

V.S.: What is your strength? Defence or...

S.P.: Defence is my strength.

V.S.: What game plans have you and your coach made for the coming tournaments?

S.P.: Game plans are made according to specific games. There is a slight issue about physical endurance and strength. So, whenever there is a discussion with Gopi sir, endurance is important, and remaining fit. The strength has to be improved.

In the morning, at 8.30, our warm up starts and 9 o' clock we start our actual session. In the morning, we mainly play on court. On Monday, Tuesday, Thursday and Friday, we do stroke practice, and on Wednesday we play games. On Saturday morning, we have a light session. There might be some massage sessions or stretching exercises in-between. From 1.30–3.30 I sleep. Then my evening starts at 4. In the evenings on Mondays and Fridays we do running sessions. Saturday, Sunday and Wednesday evenings are off; on Tuesday and Thursday we do gymming. In the gym we do squats, exercise all leg muscles and I especially do more of shoulders because there I feel the strength is less. After gymming we do some skipping, and shadows. Badminton is my life. So I have to win many big tournaments. I like getting medals in tournaments like the World Championship and the All England series etc. All the hard work that I have put in and the medals I have brought back—everything is for my country.

V.S.: Sai, badminton is regarded as the speediest in any racquet game. So I am going to ask you some questions and note how fast you can reply to them, going by your speed in the game. Are you ready?

S.P.: Yes...

V.S.: Is your greatest inspiration Gopichand or the old Hindi number, *Dhal gaya din, ho gayi shaam,* that song where Jeetendra is playing badminton (chuckles)?

S.P.: Gopichand (smiles).

V.S.: Do you want to take any actress or a player on a date?

S.P.: Anushka Shetty.

V.S.: Oh! The actress from *Baahubali*!

S.P.: Yes...*Baahubali* (smiles).

V.S.: What is the one thing that you are afraid of?

S.P.: Injuries.

V.S.: The first thought that comes to your mind when you hold the racquet in your hand.

S.P.: To perform well.

V.S.: Your passion for badminton in one line?

S.P.: An important part of my life.

V.S.: Favourite movie dialogue?

S.P.: Shahrukh Khan's in the movie *Don*, '*Don ko pakadna mushkil hee nahin, namumkin hain.*'

V.S.: Tell me something good about yourself.

S.P.: I am friendly.

V.S.: If you had one super power, what would you like it to be?

S.P.: To defeat everybody. Become a champion.

V.S.: What is your favourite shot...move, dance move (smiles naughtily)?

S.P.: Dance move (surprised)?

V.S.: No, no, I was just kidding. I am asking about your favourite shot on court.

S.P.: To hit a backhand corner cross court.

V.S.: What is your ultimate goal?

S.P.: To win a medal in the Olympics...but as the Olympics takes place after a gap of 4 years, winning major medals for India.

V.S.: Sai Praneeth is very dedicated and focused about his game. His dedication and labour has also imbued me with a new energy. I wish Sai all the very best for all coming tournaments and hope that all his dreams come true because his dream is the dream of the country. Jai Hind!

13

SHIVA THAPA

Boxing is a sport in which there is no bat or racquet. Your body is the implement as well as the arena. You have to use it as a tool to attack your opponent and also face an attack with it. In this sport both strength and courage are needed. You have to be spirited and active all the time. Boxing is a violent game which is played with a calm mind.

Boxing has always been very popular in India—players like Mary Kom and Vijender Singh have made it popular. There are many such players who have brought India medals in the Olympics, Commonwealth Games and Asian Games. One such person is the youngest Indian boxer to qualify in the Olympics—Shiva Thapa. Welcome to Umeed India, Shiva.

Virender Sehwag: Shiva, first of all, tell me why is it called a boxing 'ring' when nothing is circular here (pointing to the boxing ring and laughing).

Shiva Thapa: (laughs back) Sir, definitely—here where we are sitting is the boxing ring. This is the place where we apply all our strength and battle it out. This is the place for us.

V.S.: Shiva, in Hindi, there is a saying, '*Muh tod jawab dena*'. You have literally followed this adage in real life (laughs).

S.T.: If I have to talk about it, I will not say that I am an ace boxer. However, if one talks about punches, I am never one to step back.

V.S.: Tell me, what is your life like in Guwahati?

S.T.: Ever since my childhood I was into boxing. As a child, the time when they say friends are everything, my life was different. I believed and still believe that family comes first. I have four sisters and an elder brother who also started boxing with me. My parents were at home. There was so much love and nurturing at home that they never let me feel the lack of friends.

V.S.: Your father was a karate champion—for you that must have been a blessing because your father himself must have taught you at home.

S.T.: Absolutely!

V.S.: Why did you choose boxing? Who motivated you?

S.T.: Father taught me karate at home, and because he was an instructor, it became easy for me to pick it up. I also participated in a few state championships. I had won a silver and a gold medal. But it seemed to me that people did not know as much about karate as they did about Mike Tyson. Whenever I said I was into karate, they would ask if I wanted to become another Tyson! Look, there goes Tyson...they used to say. I did not know who Tyson was, but eventually, I came to know that Tyson was a boxer. Further, boxing was a game that was played only through punches and fists and there was no use of one's feet at all. That got me further interested in the game. But I became interested in the sport for good when I got punched and my nose started bleeding.

V.S.: This made your interest greater instead of lessening it (surprised and smiling)?!

S.T.: My interest grew because at that time my trainer in Guwahati, Mr Amar Deka sir, did not let me fight for the first 5 or 6 months—he just taught me the basic skills, like the on-guard position and what steps to take—he taught me all of that. After 6 or 7 months, he allowed me into the ring for the first time and let me fight—I was almost immediately hit by a punch and my nose began to bleed. Instantly, I was very angry, being a bit short-tempered, and I began raining punches too. I felt that...well...how can anyone hit me in this manner? These were the minute factors that led me into boxing.

V.S.: Your brother is also a boxer?

S.T.: Yes, sir.

V.S.: So when both the brothers are at home, are there fights to see who is a better boxer (smiles)?

S.T.: We never fight at home—there are very few such incidents that I can remember. There is a major reason behind this—when we are training, we fight. The little anger that remains, we finish off in the ring itself, and nobody even comes to know about it. That's one of the reasons why we continue boxing (laughs).

V.S.: What are the differences you feel between when you are practising on your own in the town of Guwahati and when you go somewhere else to practise?

S.T.: While practising in Guwahati, the family is there with me. My father is there during the training and that is a big motivation. Ever since childhood, the true motivation has been from home, and all the support has come from home.

It is very different when we are training in camps—in the Patiala camp or when we go overseas for training or competitions. The ambience is very different. I miss my family a lot when I am outside for training.

V.S.: There are periods in the life of every player when he leaves his family and home and travels to another city for practice or to play matches. There he definitely misses his family a lot. This has happened to me a number of times too, when we have gone to play outside or gone for training to the Under–19 camps, and this is also what happened to Shiva.

Do you have any childhood memories about boxing that you would like to share with us?

S.T.: Winning and losing can make a lot of difference to a player. The first defeat that I faced...I had gone to play the nationals in Noida. I lost, and there were a number of reasons for that. I was a little late and there was a slight lack of coordination about the timetable. I had not known that my opponent had reached the ring before me and I had not even reached the stadium at the time. Neither had the warm up been done nor the stretching. I just put on my shoes and entered the ring. In the first round I played well, quite well. But in the second and third rounds, because I had not warmed up, my calf muscles became stiff and the leg muscles tightened. I lost that fight.

It was my first big match on a national level and I cried a lot that day. I asked my father whether I would be able to continue with boxing or not—since my self-confidence had taken quite a beating. My father assured me that one should never pass judgement based on a single defeat. At that time, my father motivated me a great deal. That, I think, was the first incident in my life that taught me the difference between victory and defeat.

V.S.: Difficulties are part of a player's life; but in a home where the father, brother and many members are associated with sports, it becomes a lot easier to deal with the problems. That was the advantage that Shiva had. His father is a karate champion and his mother, being amidst so many boxers, must have started thinking like a player herself.

Mr and Mrs Thapa, thank you for joining us. Tell me, how was Shiva as a child?

Mrs Thapa: He was a very cool and calm person. In studies, too, he was quite good.

Mr Thapa: When boxing practice began, it was very difficult to divide time between studies and boxing. So, we would make him get up at 3 o' clock to study and then go for training.

V.S.: Has Shiva been boxing since childhood?

Mr Thapa: Yes, in the beginning he started with karate. I have played a lot of karate and body-contact games. Later I came to know that these games were not part of the Olympics, and my dream was to participate in the Olympics. So I turned him towards boxing. At that time some media persons had asked Shiva, 'If you had not become a boxer, what would you be?' Shiva thought very fast and almost immediately answered, 'This is the reason I was born.' This was after the Hyder Ali Tournament, and the media again asked him, 'Should we print what you have just said?' And he said, 'Yes, I was born to be a boxer (smiles and points to the poster of Shiva with the caption, *I was born to be a boxer*).'

V.S.: Aunty, tell me, when he used to come home after practice, sometimes after having hurt himself and sometimes even bleeding, how did you feel then?

Mrs Thapa: I have never seen his live matches. Staying at home, I pray to God, that's all. When he is hurt, there is a great fear, but there is also a belief; he is working and trying so hard for his country and making a name for himself—there is also happiness in that (smiles).

V.S.: When he is at home, what does he enjoy doing? How does he pass his time?

Mr Thapa: When Sai comes home from the camp, he trains at home in the morning, and sometimes he goes to the gym for training. He keeps up his twice-a-day training.

V.S.: He surely does something else besides training—goes for movies, chats with people? He must have a girlfriend?

Mr Thapa: I have not heard about girlfriends (smiles).

V.S.: Neither will he tell you (smiles back).

Mrs Thapa: He prefers to spend time at home. Then there are also visits to his sister's and aunt's house. Sai likes to spend time at home and listen to music. He is fond of music.

Mr Thapa: He spends most of his time at home and does not like to go out much.

V.S.: When did it occur to you that Sai might make some sort of a name in boxing?

Mr Thapa: In 2005, when the National Championship was held in Noida, he was supposed to play in Group A or B, but his weight was not appropriate. And one has to be in the correct weight band to participate in the championship. I gave him 2–3 litres of water and made him gulp down some food to increase his weight (smiles). He went on to defeat players taller than him, and even defeated the boxer from Haryana who was the best player from that state. He won 3 medals then.

Mrs Thapa: And I was the first one he called to inform that he had won a gold (big smile). He was very happy.

Mr Thapa: Then, in 2006–07, it was the Hyder Ali International Tournament, which took place in Russia—and he also won the gold there. Our hopes grew and we were almost sure that he would qualify. Then, finally, in 2012, he qualified and became the youngest Indian Olympian.

V.S.: When he played for his country for the first time, how did it feel?

Mr Thapa: It felt very good because it was my childhood dream that one day I would represent my country, but unfortunately, I never got an opportunity to do so. But when he played for his country for the first time, it felt like I was standing there on the podium and receiving the medal.

V.S.: Shiva has now become a role model for the other boys in his village. How do you feel?

Mrs Thapa: Whenever we go out, people keep asking—where is Shiva now? What is he doing?

V.S.: Has it ever happened that when you are out somewhere, people point at you, saying, 'Look, here are Shiva's parents!'?

Mr Thapa: Yes, nowadays people don't call me by my name—they call me Shiva Thapa's father (big smile)!

Mrs Thapa: We are now known by Shiva's identity (smiles).

Mr Thapa: My name is Shiva Thapa's father now. They have even saved my mobile number as 'Shiva Thapa's father'! Nobody even knows my name!

Mrs Thapa: If they see me, they will ask, 'You are Shiva's mother, aren't you?'

Mr Thapa: This is a matter of great pride for me and it is as good as getting the Olympic medal. Shiva is equally proud of his achievements...

S.T.: I feel very proud when we go outside the country and perform for the country and win medals in big events. There are so many well-wishers and they send me off with so much goodwill. When I return with medals after a good performance, it feels very good.

V.S.: Shiva, how was the excitement of representing your country at an international event?

S.T.: It felt very good, and honestly, I was not under any kind of pressure. I am saying this because usually when a player steps out of his country to play, he/she carries a burden. There was, however, no pressure on me. Yes, once I continued playing, there was pressure (smiles).

V.S.: From where did your international journey start and how has it been so far?

S.T.: My international tournaments started in 2007, with the Hyder Ali Cup in which I won gold. After that I participated in a lot of international events...in the Asia Cup I took the gold, and the bronze medal in the World Junior Championship in 2008 in Azerbaijan. My journey in youth tournaments has also been quite good. In the World Youth Championships I won the silver medal in 2010 in Singapore. It was quite a major turning point in my life. The 2012 Olympics in London was a dream for me. But I did not think that I would qualify, because at that time 18 years was the eligible age for the senior boxing group—I was then just 3 months past 18 years. So it seemed to me that without any exposure in the senior group I would not be able to perform, I was pretty young at the time—so I was not sure about myself. Because of this there was no pressure on me and I went on to qualify. Vijender Bhaisaab was also in the team with me—we had both applied for the same competition. Our competition was in Kazakhstan. So, his presence in the team definitely inspired and motivated everybody. When he played and was winning, it felt great. I was also playing and the coordination was good and we were like brothers...he also guided us during matches. So I felt that when I qualified without pressure and then won the gold medal, it was quite a good start to the London Olympics.

V.S.: You qualified for the 2012 London Olympics; tell us what your experience there was like.

S.T.: The Olympic journey from the time of qualifying was a dream come true for me. There was a lot of media coverage, so much so that the entire family was interviewed on TV (smiles). When I reached London, it was an environment which one can only dream of. You are rubbing shoulders with the likes of Usain Bolt and Michael Phelps! It was a blessed moment for me to actually meet these two legends. I met Michael Phelps for a short while but the way he wished me good luck in my games, it was surreal. I too congratulated him on his victories. There was a positive vibe all around, which was very stimulating. So the London Olympic experience was also pretty good. After that I had also targeted the Rio Olympics and was successful.

V.S.: You qualified in two Olympics back-to-back. Tell us something about that.

S.T.: I guess it is the dream of every player to qualify for the Olympics. So qualifying in two Olympics holds great meaning for me. There was a lot that I learned. If I talk about my game...in the London Olympics in my very first round I played with a boxer from Mexico who had already played two Olympics. He was quite an aggressive boxer. I was leading in the first two rounds; then, in the last round, in just a few seconds, there was a setback of 2 or 3 points, because of which I lost that game. Then, in the Rio Olympics, my match was with a Cuban boxer who was an undefeated boxer and he eventually went on to win gold in the Olympics. Even though I was defeated in these two Olympics, I learnt a lot from these encounters. I can now focus on what went wrong and improve my game.

A WEEK IN THE LIFE OF SHIVA THAPA:

The training schedule that we have consists of three sessions every day. In the morning it is for 2–2½ hours; during the day 1 hour and in the evening also it is for 2–2½ hours. From 6 in the morning to 8.30 we have the first training session. We do endurance and long endurance running; we run continuously for 6 or 7 km. Then there is the punching bag, skipping rope, gym and conditioning in the morning. During the day, the training is mostly from 10 to 11 o' clock. The training is for one hour each and is fairly individualized. In the evening, we focus on different boxing skills like sparring and school fights. In this manner the training continues from Monday to Saturday through the week. So, on some days we have strength training and on some days the focus is on endurance training. Likewise, some days we work on skill, and in this manner, every other day we have a different schedule.

My aim is to get better every day to improve in my life and to learn a lot from my mistakes.

V.S.: Is the technique for defence and attack different in boxing? If so, what do you use—defence or attack?

S.T.: Defence and aggressive attacking—both the styles are very popular in boxing. When it comes to my style, I try to fight in a very universal manner, which seems to me is my natural style. I play aggressively and also go for counter attacks; but it's not like when I am attacking I will only attack or while defending I will only defend. I mix the two and remain neutral. That is my style. In boxing parlance it is known as mid-distance boxing.

V.S.: How important is footwork in boxing and how much of it do you use?

S.T.: Float like a butterfly and sting like a bee. These are the famous words of the legendary boxer Muhammad Ali and I follow them with all my heart. Tyson does not use his footwork that much, though.

V.S.: So Tyson is like Sehwag (laughs).

S.T.: (laughs back) Yeah...Muhammad Ali's footwork can also be compared to any dance...you know the whole thing about floating like a butterfly...he was a heavy boxer of more than 100 kg but he floated in the ring and thrashed his opponents. His footwork was very light. He used to carry himself in such a light manner—so that footwork inspired me quite a lot.

V.S.: How many types of punches are there in boxing and what is your speciality?

S.T.: There are six punches in boxing—there is the left straight, right straight, left upper cut, right upper cut, hitting mostly in the belly, the left hook and the right hook. These are the 6 punches which are combined in a variety of ways, and by mixing them, we have different techniques.

V.S.: My favourite is the upper cut—but not in boxing, in cricket (laughs). Shiva, now tell me what are the ways or techniques in which a boxing match can be won?

S.T.: A very skilled player had said, 'Punch, but don't get hit.' The first rule of boxing is that you have to punch, but do not get punched. If you punch twice and then get punched twice, it is equal and the points become equal. Punch and then defend yourself as much as you can from the opponent's punches.

V.S.: So, by following these techniques, you can win?

S.T.: Definitely!

V.S.: What is you ultimate goal?

S.T.: To represent India in a stage like the Olympics, win medals and bring honour to my country. Another objective is to inspire the youth as much as I can and share my achievements with them so that they can also fulfil their dreams.

V.S.: Friends, whenever I meet such sportspersons like Shiva, I am always reminded of their reality, that even though they come from small places, their dreams are big, their goals are laudable and there is honesty and depth in their dedication. We wish Shiva brings great honours to our country—because when that happens we, too, will hold our heads high with pride. Jai Hind!